Paddington Children's Hospital

Caring for children—and captivating hearts!

The doctors and nurses of
Paddington Children's Hospital are renowned
for their expert care of their young patients,
no matter the cost. And now, as they face
both a heart-wrenching emergency
and a dramatic fight to save their hospital,
the stakes are higher than ever!

Devoted to their jobs, these talented
professionals are about to discover that saving
lives can often mean risking your heart…

Available now in the thrilling
Paddington Children's Hospital miniseries:

Their One Night Baby
by Carol Marinelli

Forbidden to the Playboy Surgeon
by Fiona Lowe

Mummy, Nurse…Duchess?
by Kate Hardy

Falling for the Foster Mum
by Karin Baine

And coming soon…

Healing the Sheikh's Heart
by Annie O'Neil

A Life-Saving Reunion
by Alison Roberts

Dear Reader,

This book has been such a rollercoaster to write—I really hope you enjoy reading my slice of life at Paddington Children's Hospital.

As excited as I was about taking part in my first continuity series, the prospect of writing along with such fabulous established authors was daunting for a newbie, to say the least! I shouldn't have worried. These ladies had such fabulous ideas for the series, and are so much better organised than I am, it made the process easier.

A book set in London was also a great excuse for a research trip—and it just so happened to coincide with my twentieth wedding anniversary! I had a lovely day at the zoo with my hubby, following in Quinn, Matt and little Simon's footsteps. Albeit in the rain…

Maybe for our silver anniversary I'll plan a research trip somewhere a bit more exotic. Surely they have doctors on Mediterranean cruises too…

Happy reading!

Karin xx

FALLING
FOR THE
FOSTER MUM

BY
KARIN BAINE

First published in Great Britain 2017
By Mills & Boon, an imprint of HarperCollins*Publishers*
1 London Bridge Street, London, SE1 9GF

Large Print edition 2017

© 2017 Harlequin Books S.A.

Special thanks and acknowledgement are given to Karin Baine for her contribution to the Paddington Children's Hospital series.

ISBN: 978-0-263-06732-3

MIX
Paper from
responsible sources
FSC
www.fsc.org   FSC™ C007454

This book is produced from independently certified FSC paper to ensure responsible forest management. For more information visit www.harpercollins.co.uk/green.

Printed and bound in Great Britain
by CPI Group (UK) Ltd, Croydon, CR0 4YY

Karin Baine lives in Northern Ireland with her husband, two sons and her out-of-control notebook collection. Her mother's and her grandmother's vast collections of books inspired her love of reading and her dream of becoming a Mills & Boon author. Now she can tell people she has a *proper* job! You can follow Karin on Twitter, @karinbaine1, or visit her website for the latest news—karinbaine.com.

Books by Karin Baine

Mills & Boon Medical Romance

French Fling to Forever
A Kiss to Change Her Life
The Doctor's Forbidden Fling
The Courage to Love Her Army Doc

Visit the Author Profile page
at millsandboon.co.uk for more titles.

This one's for Jennie, Stephen and Samantha, my London travelling companions/supervisors, because we all know I can't be trusted out on my own!

Along with John. You've always been so supportive of my writing and it's much appreciated. xx

Thanks to Catherine, Abbi and Chellie, who've helped me so much with my research.

Praise for Karin Baine

'The moment I picked up Karin Baine's debut medical romance I knew I would not be disappointed with her work. Poetic and descriptive writing, engaging dialogue, thoroughly created characters and a tightly woven plot propels *French Fling to Forever* into the must-read, highly recommended level.'

—*Contemporary Romance Reviews*

PROLOGUE

QUINN GRADY WAS officially the worst mother in the world. Barely a week into the job and her charge was already lying in the hospital.

Simon mightn't be her *real* son but that made her role as his foster mum even more important. As someone who'd been passed from pillar to post in the care system herself, it meant everything to her to provide a safe home for him. Yet here she was, sitting on her own in the bright corridors of the Paddington Children's Hospital, nerves shredded, waiting for news on his condition.

She'd done everything by the parenting handbook, even when life had thrown her that 'I'm not ready to be a dad' curveball from Darryl right before Simon had come into her life. Her focus had remained on his welfare regardless of her own heartbreak that her partner had gone back on his word that he was going into this with her. The sleepless nights she'd spent with her mind running through every possible scenario she might encounter as someone's guardian hadn't prepared her for this.

A fire at the school.

As she'd waved a tearful goodbye this morning and watched Simon walk away in his smart, new uniform she'd half expected a phone call. He'd looked so small, so lost, she'd almost been waiting for the school to call and ask her to pick him up, to come and hug him and tell him everything was going to be all right.

Not this. A fire was totally beyond her control. She couldn't have prevented it and she couldn't fix it. Apparently all she could do was fill in endless forms and she hadn't even been able to do that until she'd contacted the local fostering authority to notify them about what had happened. Watching the frantic staff deal with the influx of injured schoolchildren, she'd never felt so helpless.

She knew Simon was badly hurt but she hadn't been able to see him yet until they stabilised him. He could have life-changing injuries. Or worse. What if he didn't make it? Her stomach lurched, terror gripping her insides at the thought of his suffering. This was supposed to have been a new start for both of them, to wipe out the past and build a better future. Now all she wanted was to see him and know he was okay.

She fidgeted in the hard plastic chair doing her best not to accost any of the nurses running from department to department. Perhaps if she was a *proper* mum she'd feel more entitled to demand constant information on his condition.

'Are you Simon's mother?'

A vision in green scrubs appeared beside her. His lovely Irish lilt was the comfort blanket she needed at this moment in time.

'No. Yes.' She didn't know the appropriate response for this kind of situation.

As a pair of intense, sea-green eyes stared at her, waiting for an answer, she realised her temporary status didn't matter. 'I'm his foster mother.'

It was enough to soften the doctor's features and he hunched down beside her chair.

'I'm Matthew McGrory, a burns specialist. I've been brought over to assess Simon's condition.'

Quinn held her breath. *Good news or bad?*

She searched his face for a sign but apart from noting how handsome he was up close she discovered nothing.

'How is he?'

Good?

Bad?

'Would you like to come through and see for yourself?' The doctor's mouth tilted into a smile.

That had to be positive, right?

'Yes. Thank you.' She got to her feet though her legs weren't as steady as she needed them to be. Nonetheless she hurried down the corridor, powering hard to keep up with the great strides of a man who had to be at least six foot.

He stopped just outside the door of the Paediatric Intensive Care Unit, the last barrier between her and Simon, but an ominous one. Only the most poorly children would be on the other side and he was one of them. Not for the first time she wished she had someone to go through this with her.

'Before we go in, I want you to be prepared. Simon has suffered severe burns along with some smoke inhalation. It's not a pretty sight but everything we're doing is to minimise long-term damage. Okay? Ready?'

She nodded, feigning bravery and nowhere near ready. Whatever the injuries, they would affect her and Simon for a long time but they were in this together.

'He needs me,' she said, her voice a mere whisper as she tried to pull herself together. She wondered if clinging to the hunky doctor's arm for support was an option but he was already opening the door and stepping into the ward before she could make a grab for him.

They passed several cubicles but she couldn't make out any of the faces as the small bodies were dwarfed by monster machinery aiding their recovery.

'Oh, Simon!' Her hand flew to her mouth to cover the gasp as she was led to the last bed on the row. She wouldn't have recognised him if not for the glimpse of curly hair against the pillow.

The face of the little boy she'd left at the school gates only hours ago was now virtually obscured by the tubes and wires going in and out of his tiny form keeping him alive. His pale torso was a contrast to the mottled black and red angry skin of his right arm stretched out at his side. Lying there, helpless, he looked even younger than his meagre five years.

Quinn's knees began to buckle at the enormity of the situation and the tears she'd been desperately trying to keep at bay finally burst through the dam.

Strong hands seemed to come from nowhere to catch her before she fell to the floor in a crumpled heap of guilt and manoeuvred her into a chair.

'I know it's a lot to take in but he's honestly

in the best place. Simon has severe burns to the face and arm and we have him intubated to help him breathe after the smoke inhalation. Once the swelling has gone down and we're happy there's no damage to his eyes, we'll move him to the burns unit for further treatment.'

She blinked through her tears to focus on the man kneeling before her.

'Is he going to be okay?' That was all she needed to know.

'The next forty-eight hours will be crucial in assessing the full extent of his burns. He'll need surgery to keep the wounds clean and prevent any infection and there's a good chance he'll need skin grafts in the future. I won't deny it'll be a long process, but that's why I'm here. I'm a reconstructive surgeon too and I will do my very best to limit and repair any permanent scarring. The road to recovery is going to be tough but we're in this together.' This virtual stranger reached out and gave her hand a squeeze to reassure her but the electric touch jolted her back into reality.

She was a mum now and following in the footsteps of her own amazing adoptive mum, who'd moved heaven and earth to do what was best for her. It was time for her to step up to the plate now too.

'I'll do whatever it takes. Simon deserves the best.' And something told her that the best was surgeon Matthew McGrory.

CHAPTER ONE

Two months later

QUINN WISHED THEY did an easy-to-read, step-by-step guide for anxious foster mums going through these operations too. It was difficult to know what to do for the best when Simon resisted all attempts to comfort him pre-op.

He turned his face away when she produced the well-worn kids' book the hospital had provided to explain the surgical process.

She sighed and closed the book.

'I suppose you know this off by heart now.' Not that it made this any easier. After the countless hours he'd spent on the operating table they both knew what they were in for—pain, tears and a huge dollop of guilt on her part.

She hadn't caused the fire or his injuries but neither had she been able to save him from this suffering. Given the choice she'd have swapped places with the mite and offered herself up for this seemingly endless torture rather than watch him go through it.

'Can I get you anything?' she asked the back of his head, wishing there was something she could do other than stand here feeling inadequate.

The pillow rustled as he shook his head and she had to suppress the urge to try and swamp him into a big hug the way her mother always had when she'd been having a hard time. Simon didn't like to be hugged. In fact, he resisted any attempt to comfort him. That should've been his *real* mother's job but then apparently she'd never shown affection for anything other than her next fix. His too-young, too-addicted parents were out of the picture, their neglect so severe the courts had stripped them of any rights.

Quinn and Simon had barely got to know each other before the fire had happened so she couldn't tell if his withdrawal was a symptom of his recent trauma or the usual reaction of a foster child afraid to get attached to his latest care giver. She wasn't his parent, nor one of the efficient medical staff, confident in what they were doing. For all she knew he'd already figured out she was out of her depth and simply didn't want to endure her feeble overtures. Maybe he just didn't like her. Whatever was causing the chasm between them it was vital she closed it, and fast.

As if on cue, their favourite surgeon stepped into the room. 'Back again? I'm sure you two are sick of the sight of me.'

That velvety Irish accent immediately caught her attention. She frowned as goose bumps popped up across her skin. At the age of thirty-two she should really have better self-control over an ill-conceived crush on her foster son's doctor.

'Hi, Matt.' An also enchanted Simon sat upright in bed.

It was amazing how much they both seemed to look forward to these appointments and hate them at the same time. Although the skin grafts were a vital part of recovery, they were traumatic and led to more night terrors once they returned home as Simon relived the events of the fire in his sleep. He'd been one of the most seriously burned children, having been trapped in his classroom by falling debris. Although the emergency services had thankfully rescued him, no one had been able to save him from the memories or the residual pain.

Matt, as he'd insisted they call him, was the one constant during this whole nightmare. The one person Simon seemed to believe when he said things would work out. Probably because he had more confidence in himself and his abilities than she did in herself, when every dressing change made her feel like a failure.

The poor child's face was still scarred, even after the so-called revolutionary treatment, and his arm was a patchwork quilt of pieced together skin. Technically his injuries had occurred in school but that didn't stop her beating herself up that it had happened on her watch. Especially when the fragile bond they'd had in those early days had disintegrated in the aftermath of the fire. Unlike the one he'd forged with the handsome surgeon.

Matt moved to the opposite side of the bed from Quinn and pulled out some sort of plastic slide from his pocket. 'I've got a new one for you, Simon. The disappearing coin trick!' he said with flare, plucking a ten pence piece from the air.

'Cool!'

Of course it was. Magic was a long way away from the realities of life with second- and third-degree burns. Fun time with Matt before surgery offered an escape whilst she was always going to be the authority figure telling him not to scratch and slathering cream over him when he just wanted to be left alone.

Somehow Simon was able to separate his friend who performed magic tricks from the surgeon who performed these painful procedures, whereas she was the one he associated with his pain. It was frustrating, especially seeing him so engaged when she'd spent all day trying to coax a few words from him.

'I need you to place the coin in here.' He gave Simon the coin and pulled out a tray with a hole cut out of the centre from the plastic slide.

Concentration was etched on his face as he followed instructions and once Quinn set aside her petty jealousy she appreciated the distraction from the impending surgery. After all, that's what she wanted for him—to be the same as any other inquisitive five-year-old, fascinated by the world around him. Not hiding away, fearful of the unknown, the way he was at home.

'Okay, so we push it back in here—' he slid the tray back inside the case '—and this is the important bit. We need a magic word.'

'Smelly pants!' Simon had the mischievous twinkle of a child who knew he could get away with being naughty on this occasion.

'I was thinking along the more traditional abracadabra line but I guess that works too.' Matt exchanged a grin across the bed with her. It was a brief moment which made her forget the whole parent/doctor divide and react as any other woman who'd had a good-looking man smile at her.

That jittery, girlish excitement took her by surprise as he made eye contact with her and sent her heart rate sky high. Since Darryl left her she hadn't given any thought to the opposite sex. At least not in any 'You're hot and I want you' way. More of a 'You're a man and I can't trust you' association. She wasn't prepared to give away any more of herself—of her time or her heart— to anyone who wouldn't appreciate the gift. All of her time and energy these days was directed into the fostering process, trying to make up for the lack of two parents in Simon's life. Harbouring any form of romantic ideas was self-indulgent and, most likely, self-destructive.

She put this sudden attraction down to the lack of adult interaction. Since leaving her teaching post to tutor from home and raise Simon, apart from the drive-by parents of her students, and her elderly neighbour, Mrs Johns, the medical staff were the only grown-ups she got to talk to. Very few of them were men, and even fewer had cheekbones hand-carved by the gods. It was no wonder she'd overreacted to a little male attention. The attraction had been there since day one and she'd fought it with good reason when her last romantic interlude had crashed her world around her. Everything she'd believed in her partner had turned out to be a lie, making it difficult for her to trust a word anyone told her any more. She kept everyone at a distance now, but Matt was such a key figure in their days that he was nigh on impossible to ignore. As the weeks had gone on she found herself getting into more arguments with him, forcing him to take the brunt of her fears for Simon and the annoyance she should have directed at herself.

Matt waved his hand over the simple piece of plastic which had transformed Simon's body language in mere seconds.

'Smelly pants!' he shouted, echoed by his tiny assistant.

The magician-cum-surgeon frowned at her. Which apparently was equally as stimulating as a smile.

'It'll only work if we all say the magic words together. Let's try this again.'

Quinn rolled her eyes but she'd go along with

anything to take Simon's mind off what was coming next.

'Smelly pants!' they all chorused as Matt pulled out the now empty tray.

'Wow! How did you do that?' Simon inspected the magic chamber, suitably impressed by the trick.

'Magic.' Matt gave her a secret wink and started her tachycardia again.

Didn't he have theatre prep or intensive hand-scrubbing to do rather than showing off here and disturbing people's already delicate equilibrium?

'I wish I could make my scars disappear like that.' Simon's sudden sad eyes and lapse back into melancholy made Quinn's heart ache for him.

'I'm working on it, kiddo. That's why all of these operations are necessary even though they suck big-time. It might take a few waves of my magic wand but I'll do my very best to make them disappear.'

Quinn folded her arms, binding her temper inside her chest. He might mean well but he shouldn't be giving the child false hope. Simon's body was a chequered, vivid mess of dead and new flesh. He was never going to have blemish-free skin again, regardless of the super-confident surgeon's skills, and she was the one who'd have to pick up the pieces when the promises came to nothing. Again.

'You said that the last time.' Not even Simon was convinced, lying back on the bed, distraction over.

'I also said it would take time. Good things come to those who wait, right?' It was a mantra he'd used since day one but he clearly wasn't *au fait* with the limited patience of five-year-olds. Unlike Quinn, who'd had a crash course in tantrums and tears while waiting for the miraculous recovery to happen before her very eyes. Her patience had been stretched to the limit too.

'Right,' Simon echoed without any conviction.

'I'll tell you what, once you're back from theatre and wide awake, I'll come back and show you how to do a few tricks of your own. Deal?'

Quinn couldn't tell if it was bravado or ego preventing the doctor from admitting defeat as he stood with his hand held out to make the bargain. Either way, she didn't think it was healthy for him to get close to Simon only to let him down. He'd had enough of that from his birth parents, who'd given up any rights to him in favour of drugs, foster parents, who'd started the adoption process then abandoned him when they'd fallen pregnant themselves, and her, who'd sent him to get burned up in school. It might have failed her once but that protective streak was back with a vengeance.

'We couldn't ask you to do that. I'm sure you have other patients to see and we've already taken up so much of your time.' She knew these extra little visits weren't necessary. They had highly skilled nurses and play specialists to make these transitions easier for the children. These informal chats and games made her feel singled out. As if he was trying to suss out her capability to look after Simon outside of the hospital. The nurses had noticed too, remarking how much extra time he'd devoted to Simon's recovery and she didn't appreciate it as much as they probably thought she should. He wasn't going to sneak his way into her affections the way Darryl had, then use her fostering against her; she'd learned that lesson the hard way. She could do this. Alone.

'Not at all. I'm always willing to pass on my secrets to a budding apprentice.' He held out his hand again and Simon shook it with his good arm, bypassing her concerns.

'I just mean perhaps you should be concentrating on the surgery rather than performing for us.' The barb was enough to furrow that brow again but he had a knack for getting her back up. Handsome or not, she wouldn't let him cause Simon any more pain than necessary.

The wounded look in his usually sparkling green eyes instantly made her regret being such a cow to him when he'd been nothing but kind to Simon since the accident. His smile was quickly back in place but it no longer reached anywhere past his mouth.

'It's no problem. I can do both. I'll see you

soon, kiddo.' He ruffled Simon's hair and turned to leave. 'Can I have a word outside, Ms Grady?'

As he brushed past her, close enough to whisper into her ear, Quinn's whole body shivered with awareness. A combination of nerves and physical attraction. Neither of which she had control over any longer.

'Sure,' she said although she suspected he wasn't giving her a choice; she felt as though she was being called into the headmaster's office for misbehaving. A very hot headmaster who wasn't particularly happy with her. Unsurprising, really, when she'd basically just insulted him on a professional level.

She promised Simon she'd be back soon and took a deep breath before she followed Matt out the door.

'I know you're having a tough time at the moment but I'd really appreciate it if you stopped questioning my dedication to my job in front of my patient.'

It was the first time Quinn had seen him riled in all of these weeks. He was always so calm in the face of her occasional hysteria, so unflappable through every hurdle of Simon's treatment. Although it was unsettling to see the change in him, that intense passion, albeit for his work, sent tingles winding through her body until her toes curled, knowing she was the one who'd brought it to the fore. She found herself wondering how deep his passions lay and how else they might manifest...

He cleared his throat and reminded her she was supposed to speak, to argue back. She questioned what he was doing, he pulled her up on it and claimed rank when it came to Simon's health care—that was the way this went. It kept her from going completely round the bend imagining the worst that could happen when she'd be the one left dealing with the consequences on her own. She was supposed to be the overprotective mother voicing her concerns that everything being done was in her son's best interests, just as he was the one to insist he knew what he was doing. Fantasising about Matt in any other capacity, or his emotions getting the better of him, definitely wasn't in their well-rehearsed script.

'Yeah…well…I'd appreciate it if you didn't give Simon false hope that everything will go back to normal. We've both had enough of people letting us down.' Not that she knew what normal was, but although he deserved a break, they had to be realistic too.

'I'm not in the habit of lying to my patients…'

'No? What about this miracle spray-on skin which was supposed to fast-track his recovery? It's been two months and his burns are still very much visible. I should've known it was too good to be true when you would only use it to treat his facial burns and not the ones on his arm. I mean, if it was such a wonder cure it would make sense to use it everywhere and not make him go through these skin grafts anyway.' She was aware her voice had gone up a few decibels and yet she couldn't seem to stop herself when something good she'd believed was going to happen hadn't. This time it wasn't only *her* hopes that were being dashed.

Matt simply sighed when Quinn would've understood if he'd thrown his hands up and walked away. Deep down she knew he'd done his best, and yet, they were still here going through the same painful process.

'I can only reiterate what I told you at the start. It will take time. Perhaps the progress we have made isn't as noticeable to you because you see him every day, but the scars *are* beginning to fade. It's as much as we can hope for at this stage. As I explained, this is a new treatment, not readily available everywhere in the UK, and funding is hard to come by. The burns on Simon's arm are full thickness, not suitable for the trial, otherwise I'd have fought tooth and nail to make it happen. But he's young—his skin will heal quicker than yours or mine. Besides, I'm good at what I do.' There wasn't any obvious arrogance in his words or stance. It was simply a statement of fact. Which did nothing to pull her mind out of the gutter.

'So you keep telling me,' she muttered under her breath. However, despite his conscientious efforts, Simon no longer resembled the child she'd been charged with minding, either physically or mentally.

'I meant what I said. I'm not in the habit of lying to sick kids, or their beautiful mothers.' His forehead smoothed out as he stopped being cross with her.

The renewed smile combined with the reassuring touch of his hands on her shoulders sent those shivers back Irish dancing over her skin. She was too busy squealing inside at the compliment to correct him again about being Simon's *foster* mother.

Unfortunately, in her experience she couldn't always take people's word as truth. It wasn't that long ago Darryl had sworn he was in this thing with her.

'I hope not,' she said, the cold chill moving to flatten the first fizz of ardour she'd felt since her ex abandoned her and the future they'd planned together.

Simon's fate was entirely in this man's hands. Matt's skills on the operating table would determine his long-term appearance and probably his self-esteem along with it. It was too much to expect her to put her faith entirely in the word of a virtual stranger. Especially when the men closest to her had littered her life with broken promises and dreams.

Quinn Grady was a grade-A pain in the backside. In the most understandable way. Matt had seen his fair share of anxious parents over the years. His line of work brought people to him in their most fragile, vulnerable state and it was only natural that emotions ran high, but she'd spent most of the last couple of months questioning his every decision, seemingly doubting his ability to get Simon through the other side of his injuries. It was exhausting for all of those concerned. Normally he outlined his treatment plan and got on with it but somehow this case had drifted off course.

The spray-on skin was a relatively new treatment. Instead of these painful skin grafts, a small sample of healthy skin was removed from the patient and placed in a processing unit where it reproduced in a special suspension solution which was then sprayed over the damaged area where it continued to grow and multiply. There was no risk of the patient's body rejecting it because it was from the patient's own cells. The regenerative nature of this process meant the wounds healed rapidly in comparison to traditional techniques, such as the one he was performing now. If it wasn't for the extensive burns on Simon's arm, where he'd defended himself from the flames, he wouldn't have to go through the skin grafts or worry about scarring because the spray-on skin would stretch with him as he grew.

He'd expected Quinn to be wary; he'd had to convince her as well as the board that this was worth trialling, but the constant clashing had tested him. Naturally, she wanted instant results, for the burns to fade and heal overnight, but that wasn't how it worked. Almost every day she demanded to know 'Why?' and he couldn't always give her the answer she wanted. *He* knew the results were favourable compared to some he'd seen, and indeed, Simon's facial burns were exceptionally better healed than those on his arm but he was still disfigured. For now. Until the boy resembled his pre-fire self, Matt was going to take the flak, and so far he'd been happy to do so.

He knew he'd probably become too involved with Simon's case, more so than the other children he'd seen at Paddington's as a result of the fire at Westbourne Grove Primary School. Perhaps it was because his burns had been so extensive, or perhaps the reason was closer to home. The single foster mum reminded him a lot of himself and the hand he'd been dealt once upon a time.

Although he assumed she'd voluntarily agreed to take on the responsibility for other people's children. His role as a stand-in father had been thrust upon him when his dad had died and left him in charge of his younger siblings.

Matt recognised the fear in Quinn's brilliant blue eyes, even when she was giving him grief. He'd spent over a decade fretting about getting his sisters through their childhood in one piece with much the same haunted expression staring back at him in the mirror.

It was only now that Bridget, the youngest of the brood, had gone off to university he was able to relax a little. Of course, that didn't mean he wasn't still handling relationship woes or doling out crisis loans, but at least he could do most of his parenting over the phone these days, unless they came to visit him in London.

It meant he had his life back, that he'd been able to leave Dublin and take this temporary contract. When his time was up here he would have no reason to feel guilty about moving on to somewhere shiny and new and far from Ireland.

Quinn wouldn't have that luxury for a long time with Simon being so young. As his foster mother, she was probably under even more pressure to get him through his injuries, and naturally, that had extended to his surgeon. If fostering authorities were anything like social services to deal with, she'd have to jump through hoops to prove her suitability as a parent.

Life was tough enough as a substitute parent

without the added trauma of the fire for her and Simon. Especially when she appeared to be doing this on her own. He hadn't spotted a wedding ring, and to his knowledge there hadn't been any other visitors during Simon's hospitalisation. When the cancer had claimed his father, Matt had been in much the same boat and being a sounding board for Quinn's frustrations was the least he could do to help. Unless her comments were in danger of unnecessarily upsetting Simon.

A boy needed a strong mother as much as a father. Matt's had been absent since shortly after Bridget's birth, when she'd suddenly decided family life wasn't for her. With his father passing away only a few years later, there had been no one left for them to turn to. For him to turn to. He'd had to manage the budget, the bills, the parent/teacher meetings and the numerous trips to A&E which were part and parcel of life with a brood of rambunctious kids, all on his own. Most of the time it had felt as though the world was against him having a life of his own.

He knew the struggle, the loneliness and the

all-encompassing fear of screwing up and he would've gone out of his way to help anyone in a similar situation. At least, that's how he justified his interest. It wasn't entirely down to the fact he enjoyed seeing her, or the sparks created every time they had one of their 'discussions.' Attraction to single mothers wasn't something he intended to act upon and certainly not with the parent of one of his patients.

He'd only just gained his freedom from one young family and he wasn't ready, willing or able to do it again. As it was, he would be in young Simon's life for a long time to come. Perhaps even longer than Quinn. There were always going to be more surgeries as the child grew and his skin stretched. Treatments for scar tissue often took months to be effective and new scar contractures, where the skin tightened and restricted movement, could appear a long way down the line in young patients who were still growing.

'He's out.' The anaesthetist gave the go-ahead for the team to begin.

Time was of the essence. Generally they didn't

keep children under the anaesthetic for more than a few hours at a time in case it proved too much for their small bodies to cope with. Hence why the skin grafts were still ongoing months later. Before they could even attempt the graft they had to clean the wound and harvest new skin from a separate donor site.

And Quinn wondered why recovery was taking so long.

'Saline, please. Let's get this done as quickly and accurately as we can.' Despite all the support in the operating theatre from the assisting staff, Matt had never borne so much responsibility for a patient as he did now.

Simon was completely at his mercy lying here, lost among the medical equipment surrounding the operating table. The slightest slip and Matt would have to face the wrath of the Mighty Quinn.

He smiled beneath his surgical mask at the thought of her squaring up to him again, her slight frame vibrating with rage as the mama bear emerged to protect her cub. She was a firebrand when she needed to be, not afraid of voicing her opinion if she thought something wasn't right. Matt didn't take offence; he was confident in the decisions he made on his patient's behalf and understood Quinn's interference came from a place of love. That didn't mean he wanted to give her further reason to berate him or challenge his authority.

He was as focused as he could be as they debrided Simon's wounds, cleaning and removing the dead tissue to clear the way for the new graft so it would take. As always, he was grateful for his perfect eyesight and steady hands as he shaved the thin slices of tissue needed for the graft. His precision as he prepared this skin before placing it on the wound could impact on Simon for the rest of his life.

No pressure.

Just two vulnerable and emotional souls relying on him to work his magic.

CHAPTER TWO

IF WAITING WAS an Olympic event, Quinn would never make it through the qualifying rounds.

Although she'd had enough experience to know to come prepared, she hadn't been able to sit still long enough to read her book or make any lesson plans for her tutored students. She'd even added an extra body to the picket line outside to save this hospital from closure in the hope it would take her mind off Simon going under the knife again. It was hard to believe anybody thought it was a good idea to merge this place with another outside the city when so many walked through the doors every day, and she was happy to wave a placard if it meant Simon's treatment continued here without any disruption.

The kids called it the Castle because of the beautiful architecture, and the story-like turrets and spires certainly gave it more character than any modern glass building could hope to replicate. Quinn had actually found it quite an imposing place at first but that could have been because of what she'd had to face inside the walls. These days it had almost become their second home and the people within were now all so familiar she didn't want anything to change.

'How's Simon?'

'You poor thing…'

'And you're out here? With us?'

'Have you heard how Ryan Walker is?'

'He's still an inpatient. I don't think there's been any real improvement. Even if he gets to go home I think the family are going to need a lot of help.'

'And they have a toddler to look after too. It's such a burden for them. For you too, Quinn, with Simon.'

The other Westbourne Grove Primary parents on the picket line had been well-meaning but the chit-chat hadn't helped her paranoia. Ryan, who'd suffered a serious head injury during the fire, was still critical and he and Simon were among the last of the children still receiving treatment. The raised eyebrows and exchanged glances at her presence anywhere other than Simon's bedside made her wonder if she had done the right thing in participating in the event and she'd abandoned her post in a hurry. Perhaps a *real* mother would've acted differently when her son was in surgery and she worried people would think she wasn't compassionate when that couldn't have been further from the truth.

That little boy meant everything to her. He might only be with her for a short time but she was as invested in him as if he was her own flesh and blood. All she wanted was for him to feel safe and loved and she'd failed on both accounts, if his continued apathy towards her was anything to go by. Perhaps when these operations became less frequent, and without the constant disruption of hospital appointments, they might actually find the time and space to bond.

She tossed her uneaten, soggy ham sandwich back into the crumpled aluminium foil. Not even the chocolate biscuit nestled in her pre-packed lunchbox could tempt her into eating. She had no appetite for anything other than news on Simon's condition. It might be a standard procedure for the staff but she knew there were risks for any surgery under general anaesthetic—breathing difficulties, adverse reaction to medication, bleeding—she'd done her Internet research on them all. Of course, none of these had occurred thus far but that didn't mean they *couldn't* happen.

In a world so full of danger she wondered how any parent ever let their offspring over the doorstep alone. It was taking all of her courage just to let Simon get the treatment recommended by the experts. At the end of the day, parental responsibility had been handed over to her and it was her job to keep him safe until adoption took place with another family.

That permanent knot in her stomach didn't untangle even when she saw him safely wheeled back onto the ward.

'How did it go?' she asked the first person who

walked through the doors towards her. Of course that person had to be Matt.

Deep down she was grateful; the surgeon was the best person to keep her informed. It was just...he was always here, disturbing her peace of mind, reminding her he was doing a better job of taking care of Simon than she was.

Matt saw no reason to prolong Quinn's misery any longer. 'It all went well. No complications or unforeseen problems. Now we just have to wait for this young man to come around again.'

It had been a long day for him with surgery and his outpatient clinic but Quinn had every right to be kept in the loop and he'd wanted to end the day on a high for all of them by coming to speak to her. He wanted to be the one to smooth out the worry lines on her brow. Besides, he'd rather she torture him for information than take out her frustrations on the rest of the staff. He could handle it better because he understood it better. After being thrown in at the deep end and having to learn on the job, he hadn't exactly

been a model parent either when he'd fought his
siblings' battles.

'Thank goodness.'

The fleeting relief across her face and the
glimpse of the pretty, young woman beneath the
mask of combative parent was Matt's reward for
a job well done.

She followed the bed into the private cubicle
with him, never letting go of Simon's hand although he was still drowsy from the anaesthetic.

'Once he comes around and he's ready for
home, we'll make sure you have painkillers to
take with you. If there's any further problem with
itching or infection let us know.'

'I think I've got the number on speed dial,' she
said with the first sign of humour of the day.

Matt knew they'd been through this routine
countless times but it was part of his duty to
make sure the correct treatment was followed up
at home. Quinn's co-operation was just as important as his in the recovery.

'As usual, we'll need you to try and keep the
dressings dry until you come back to have them

changed. You've got an appointment with the child psychologist too, right? It's important that Simon has help to process everything he's going through.' Never mind the fire itself, the surgery alone could be traumatic enough for someone so young to get past. He already seemed so withdrawn and Matt wanted to make sure they were doing all they could as a team to make him better.

'The psychologist, the physiotherapist, the dietitian—we've got a full house in appointment bingo.' Her voice was taking on that shrill quality which was always an indication of an impending showdown.

'I know it's a lot to take on but it won't be for ever. It's all to ensure Simon recovers as quickly and effectively as possible so you can both go back to your normal routine outside of these hospital walls.' He didn't know what that included since she seemed to spend every waking moment here. Almost as if she was afraid to go home.

These days he had an entirely different outlook on his personal time. There was nothing he loved more than reclaiming the peace and quiet of his apartment and the freedom of doing whatever he felt like without having to fit around other people's schedules.

'Don't.' Her small plea reached in and squeezed his insides, making him wonder how on earth he'd managed to upset her in such a short space of time.

'Don't what?' He didn't understand the sudden change in her body language as she let go of Simon's hand to wrap her arms around her waist in self-comfort.

'Don't make any more promises you have no way of keeping.'

Matt frowned. He was supposed to be the harbinger of good news, not enemy number one. 'Ms Grady, Quinn, I've assured you on many, many occasions we are doing everything in our control—'

'I've heard it all before but there always seems to be one thing after another—infections, fevers, night terrors, haemo-wotsit scars—'

'Hemotrophic.'

'Whatever. Life is never going to be *normal*

when every surgery creates further problems.' Her voice, now reaching levels only dogs and small unconscious children could hear, brought a murmur from Simon before he drifted off to sleep again.

This wasn't the time or the place for one of her dressing-downs about how nothing he did was good enough. Venting or not, Simon didn't need to hear this.

He placed a firm hand under Quinn's elbow and, for the umpteenth time since they'd met, he guided her out of the room. Whatever was going on he couldn't continually let her undermine him in front of his patient. If Simon didn't believe he could help him he might lose hope altogether.

Quinn dug her heels in but it only took a pointed glance back at the bed and an extra push to get her moving again.

'I'm not a child,' she insisted, shaking him off.

'Then stop acting like one. This is a conversation that needs to be held away from impressionable young ears.' His own temper was starting to bubble now. Why couldn't she see he would do anything to help them? She seemed determined to make this situation more difficult than it already was. Perhaps it was time he did back off if his presence here was partly to blame for getting her riled. Once he'd said his piece today he'd go back to his official role of reconstructive surgeon and nothing more.

She huffed into the corridor for another round of their battle of wills. He waited until the door was firmly closed behind them and there was no audience to overhear what he was about to say.

'The graft was a success. That's what you should be focusing on here.'

'That's easy for you to say. You're not the one he runs away from crying when it's time to bathe him, or the one who has to rock him back to sleep when he wakes from the nightmares, screaming.' Quinn's eyes were shimmering with tears, the emotions of the day clearly coming to a head.

He kept an eye out for a female member of staff who'd be in a better position to comfort her. For him to hug her was stretching the boundaries of his professionalism a tad too far. Whilst he sympathised, at the end of the day, she wasn't one of his siblings and not his direct responsibility.

'Perhaps it would help to talk to one of the other parents? I know they're bound to be going through the same struggles right now.' He didn't doubt she was having a tough time of it personally but he really wasn't the one to guide her through it.

This was why he should treat all patients exactly the same and not let sentiment, or physical attraction to a parent, cloud his judgement.

'They probably are but I'm not part of the *clique*. I'm the new kid on the block as much as Simon. Most of them have known each other for years through the Parent Teacher Association and I haven't even been around long enough to organise a playdate for Simon, much less myself. Even if I did, I'd probably have to make sure they all had background checks done first. Not the way to start any budding friendship, I'm sure you'll agree. No, we've managed this far on our own without inviting strangers in to witness our misfortune. I think we can persevere a little longer.'

She was insisting she could go it alone but those big blue eyes said otherwise and prevented Matt from walking away when he knew that was the best thing he could do to save himself.

'The staff here will always be available for you and Simon but I do think perhaps our personality clash isn't helping your stress levels. Unless there are any complications I'm sure the nurses can take care of you until the next scheduled surgery. I'll make sure I keep my promise to him today though. I will come back when he's awake and show him that magic trick.'

This time he did manage to move his feet, but as he took a step away, Quinn took one closer.

'Oh, yeah. It's so easy for you to gain his trust. A few stupid magic tricks and he thinks you're the best thing since sliced bread, but me? He hates me. I've given up my job, lost my partner and abandoned any hope of a social life so I could focus on fostering, and for what? I've failed at that too.'

The thing he'd been dreading most finally happened. The dam had burst and Quinn was weeping onto his scrubs. There was no possibility of him leaving her now. She needed a shoulder to cry on and it was simply rotten luck for both of them—he'd been the wrong person at the wrong time.

'He doesn't hate you. You're in a…transition period. That's all. After all of the trauma it's going to take a while for him to settle down.' He heard the chatter of passers-by and took it upon himself to reposition Quinn so she was against the wall and his body was shielding her from view. She was so slight in his arms, so fragile, it was a natural instinct to want to protect her.

As if he didn't have enough responsibilities in his life.

She shook against him, her sobs wracking so hard through her petite frame he was afraid she might break.

'I. Wish. I. Was. More. Like. You,' she hiccupped against his chest.

'I've never performed a sex change and I think it might be weird if I started making clones of myself.' He wanted to add that it would be a shame to tamper with the beautiful body she'd been given but it sounded inappropriate even in a joke. He wasn't supposed to be thinking about her soft curves pressed against him right now in anything other than a sympathetic and completely professional manner.

The sobbing stopped and she lifted her head from his chest, either because she'd rediscovered her sense of humour or he'd completely creeped her out. He held his breath until he read her face and exhaled when he saw the wobbly smile start to emerge.

'I mean, you're a natural with Simon, with all the kids. I'm starting to think I'm not cut out for parenthood.' Her bottom lip began to quiver again in earnest and Matt made it his personal mission to retrieve that smile.

He tilted her chin up with his thumb so she stopped staring at the floor to look at him instead. She needed to believe what he was telling her. Believe in herself.

'I've picked up a few child-wrangling tips along the way. Parenting isn't easy and that parent/child bond simply needs a little nurturing. I have a few short cuts I can share with you if you promise never to breathe a word of my secrets. I would hate to dent my reputation as the resident child-whisperer.'

'Heaven forbid. I'm sure that would break the hearts of many around here who worship the ground you walk on.' She blinked away the tears and for a split second it would be easy for Matt to forget where he was and do something stupid.

If they weren't standing in a hospital corridor he might've imagined they were having 'a moment.' She'd made it clear she wasn't one of his devoted followers and yet her body language at present said entirely the opposite.

Matt's stomach growled, a reminder he hadn't eaten anything substantial since mid-morning, and distracted him from her dilated pupils and those swollen pink lips begging him to offer some comfort. He couldn't go back on his word to help but he did need a timeout to regain his composure and remember who he was. That definitely wasn't supposed to be a man prepared to cancel a hot date in order to spend some unpaid overtime counselling families.

'Listen, there's a pub across the road—the Frog and Peach. Why don't I meet you over there in ten minutes to talk things over? We can grab a drink or a bite to eat and come straight back here the minute Simon wakes up.' There was nearly always a contingent from the hospital propping up the bar at the end of their shift and he was counting on someone else to jump in and come to Quinn's aid before he committed to something else he'd come to regret. The phone call he was going to have to make would end his most recent love interest before it even began.

She gave a wistful glance at the room behind her before she answered. The sign of a true mother thinking of her son before herself, even though she didn't realise it.

'I'll leave word to contact us the second he opens his eyes.' He wasn't going to beg but he did want to fulfil his obligations ASAP so he could finish his working day and head home. Alone.

'Only if you're sure…' Her hesitation was as obvious in her doe-like eyes as it was in her voice.

Matt wasn't any more certain this was a good idea than Quinn but a chat in a pub had to be infinitely safer than another five minutes with her in his arms.

CHAPTER THREE

QUINN SCROLLED THROUGH her phone, paying little attention to the social media updates on the screen. She wasn't in contact with any of these people; they weren't part of her *actual* life. Recent events had proved that to her. Virtual acquaintances could be chock-full of sympathy and crying emoticons on the Internet but a distinct lack of physical support from anyone other than Mrs Johns next door had made her see an online presence was a waste of her valuable time. This sudden interest in what people were having for dinner, or who had the cutest kitten meme, was simply to occupy her hands and give the impression she was at ease on her own.

Matt had directed her towards the pub across the road and assured her he'd be with her as soon as he could get away. The Frog and Peach, as nice as it was, was a busy hub in Paddington and she was self-conscious sitting outside, occupying one of the much sought after tables.

She envied the carefree patrons meeting their friends to toast the end of their working day. It reminded her of the camaraderie she'd once had with her fellow teachers inside and outside of the school. A friend was the one thing she was desperately missing right now—someone she could share a laugh with, or pour her heart out to without judgement. Mrs Johns was the closest thing to that, volunteering to babysit if she ever needed a hand, but it wasn't the kind of relationship where she could really confide everything that was getting her down at the minute. She only really had her mum to talk to on the end of the phone for that, but even then she was almost ashamed to be totally honest about her situation and admit she wasn't coping when her mother had been her fostering inspiration. When she did return home to her Yorkshire roots, she wanted it to be a journey of triumph with Simon as happy as she'd been as a child who'd finally settled.

Quinn drained the water from her glass. After the day she'd had fretting over the surgery and making a fool of herself crying on Matt's shoulder, she could probably do with something stronger but she wouldn't touch alcohol while Simon was under her care. She took her responsibilities seriously and she couldn't sit here getting pie-eyed when she still had to get them both home across the city.

'Are you finished?' A male member of staff was at her side before she managed to set the empty glass down.

She nodded but felt the need to explain her continued occupation of valuable drinking space. 'I'm just waiting for someone.'

There was a brief flicker of something replacing the irritability in the young man's eyes and Quinn's cheeks burned as she realised it was sympathy. He thought she'd been stood up. It was the natural assumption, she supposed, as opposed to her waiting for her foster son's surgeon, who she'd emotionally tortured until he'd agreed to meet her here.

'I'm sure he'll be here any minute.' She began to defend her party-of-one residency but the busy waiter had already moved on to clean the next table, uncaring about her social life, or lack of one.

Unfortunately, the jitterbugs under her skin weren't entirely down to her anticipation of an evening in a hot doctor's company. The excitement of a singleton let loose in the city didn't last for ever and these days the skippety-hop of her heart tended to come from fear of what was going to happen to Simon next.

Still, as Matt finally came into view across the street there was a surge of girlish glee she'd imagined had vanished out the door with her ex. There was something about seeing him in his casual clothes that felt forbidden, naughty even. She was so used to him in his formal shirt and trousers combo, or his scrubs, that a pair of jeans and tight T-shirt seemed more...intimate.

There was something voyeuristic watching him negotiate the traffic, oblivious to her ogling. It was amazing how one scrap of plain material became so interesting when stretched across the right body, marking out the planes of a solid chest and rounding over impressive biceps. As he jogged across the road, with his jacket slung over his arm, Matt had no clue how good he looked.

Long-dormant butterflies woke from their slumber, mistaking the handsome man coming towards Quinn as a potential date, and fluttered in her stomach as she followed his progress. They quickly settled when she turned to check her reflection in the window and was reminded this was more of a pity party than a hook-up.

She knew the second he spotted her in the crowd on the pavement as a smile spread across his lips and he lifted a hand to wave. He'd been incredibly understanding considering her sometimes erratic behaviour and this was above and beyond the call of duty, It also did nothing to diminish her crush.

'Hey,' he said as he pushed his way through to reach her table, the last of the evening sun shining behind him and lighting his short blond hair into a halo. It made him almost angelic, if it wasn't for that glint in his ever shifting blue-green eyes which said there was potential for mischief there. It made her curious to find out if there was a wicked side to Saint Matt when he was off duty.

'Hi, Matt.' She pulled out a chair for him and couldn't resist a smug grin as the surly waiter passed by and did a double take.

'Do you want to go inside to order? The smokers tend to congregate out here...unless you'd prefer that?'

'It's okay, I'm not a smoker.' It earned him more Brownie points too—as if he needed them—he obviously didn't approve of the habit.

She popped her phone back in her bag and got up to follow him. It was easy to see him when he was head and shoulders above most of the crowd, but soon the mass of bodies was too thick for her to fight through to reach him.

'Excuse me...sorry...can I just get past?'

On the verge of giving up and heading back out for some fresh air, she felt a large hand clamp around her wrist and pull her through the people forest. Somehow she ended up taking the lead with Matt creating a force field around her with his body alone. She revelled in that brief moment of nurturing where someone put her welfare first. It had been a long time since anyone had been protective of her feelings and she missed that kind of support.

Since moving away from home it had been in rare supply at all. Even Darryl, who she'd thought she'd spend the rest of her days with raising children, had put his selfish needs before her or any potential foster kids.

'There's a table over here.' Matt cleared away the dirty dishes left behind by the previous occupants so they could take the comfy leather sofas by the fire. He obviously wasn't the sort of man who only thought of himself. It showed in his every action. Even if her jealousy had prevented her from appreciating the extra care he'd given to Simon, Matt's generous nature would make some lucky woman very happy indeed. A woman who wouldn't second-guess his every gesture, waiting to find out what ulterior motive lay behind it.

'I'm sorry I've been such a nuisance.' She leaned forward in the chair, taking a sudden interest in the patina of the wooden table, unable to meet Matt's eyes. It would be fair to say she'd been an absolute horror to him these past weeks. Now the hysteria had subsided and the voice of reason had restored calm, her bad behaviour became very apparent. Based on her past experience with men, her paranoia had led her to question his judgement, his professionalism and his methods when the man had simply been trying to do his job. It was a wonder he hadn't called security to remove her from the premises at any point. His patience clearly stretched further than hers.

'Don't worry. You're an anxious mum. I get it.' He reached across the table and squeezed her hand, pumping the blood in her veins that bit faster.

She flashed her eyes up at him, surprised at the soft warmth of his touch and the very public display of support. Matt met her gaze and there was a connection of solidarity and something…

forbidden, which both comforted and confused the hell out of her.

'Are you ready to order?'

At the sound of an intruder, they sprang apart, the moment over, but the adrenaline continued surging through Quinn's body as though they'd been caught doing something they shouldn't. She began to wonder if the gum-chewing waiter was stalking her, or was more interested in her date.

Doctor. Friend. Not date.

'I…er…I'll have the burger and fries.' Matt snatched up the menu and barely glanced at it before ordering. She could read into that by saying he was as thrown by his actions as she was, or he simply ate here a lot.

'The chicken salad wrap, please.' Her appetite had yet to fully re-emerge since the fire but it would be nice to sit and enjoy a meal in company. In Matt's company. Except he was on his feet and following the waiter back towards the bar.

'I should've ordered drinks. I'll go and get some. Wine? Beer? Soft drink?' He called from an increasing distance away from her, walking backwards, bumping into furniture and generally acting as though he couldn't wait to get away from her.

Second-thoughts syndrome. He'd probably only suggested doing this to prevent another scene at his place of work.

'Just water, please.' She sighed, and slouched back in her chair, whatever spark she'd imagined well and truly extinguished.

A romantic interest from any quarter was nothing more than a fantasy these days anyway. She was going through enough emotional turmoil without leaving herself open to any more heartache. No, she should be grateful for what this was—a meal in adult company and a short respite from her responsibilities. Simon would be awake soon enough and the next round of anxious parenting would begin.

As she took in her new surroundings from her place of safety in the corner, she supposed it was a nice enough place. It had old-fashioned charm—Victorian, she guessed from the dark wood interior—and not the sort of establishment which immediately sprang to mind for a well-heeled surgeon. Matt was young, fashionable and, from what she could see, totally unencumbered by the ties she was bound by. Not that she regretted any of her choices, but if their roles were reversed she'd probably be living it up in some trendy wine bar hoping for a Matt clone to walk through the door and make her night. By weeping her way to a dinner invitation she'd no doubt spoiled the night for many single ladies across the city waiting for him to show.

'The food shouldn't be too long.' Matt took a seat opposite and placed a jug of iced water and two glasses on the table between them.

At least his agitation seemed to have passed as he poured the water with a steady hand. He was probably saving the heavy drinking for whenever he got rid of her and he could cut loose without having to babysit her.

'So...you were going to give me a tutorial in basic child-rearing...'

They may as well get this over with when they knew they both had other places to be. Ten minutes of him telling her where she was going wrong and they could all get back to their real lives, which, for her, generally didn't include pub dinners with handsome men. It was the highlight of an otherwise fraught day, it had to be said.

'Hey, I never claimed to be an expert. All I can do is pass on the benefit of my experience in dealing with young children in very trying circumstances.'

'All suggestions for helping gain a five-year-old's trust will be gratefully received.' As was the arrival of her dinner. Although she hadn't been hungry up until now, it was infinitely more appetising than the sandwich she'd binned earlier, and it was a nice change from potato smiley faces and alphabet spaghetti which were the only things Simon would eat at present.

'A cheap magic set,' Matt managed to get out before he took a huge bite out of his loaded burger. He attacked it with such a hunger it gave Quinn chills. There was more than a hint of a wild thing lurking beneath that gentlemanly exterior and a glimpse of it was enough to increase her appetite for more than the bland safe option she'd chosen.

'Pardon?'

She had to wait until he'd swallowed for an answer.

'I use bribery as a way in. I keep a box of child-friendly toys in my office for emergencies. Toy cars, colouring books, bubbles…I've even got a couple of hand puppets I break out when they're too shy to speak directly to me. I find being a friend makes the whole experience less traumatic for them.' He snagged a couple of fries from the plate and tossed them into his mouth, making short work of them too before she'd even taken her first bite.

'Tried that. He's got a room full of new toys at my place but apparently you can't buy your way into a child's heart. I think you've just got a knack with kids that apparently I don't.' It was something she'd assumed would happen naturally since she'd been in the system herself and could relate to the circumstances which would bring foster children to her.

Unfortunately, she was finding it took more than enthusiasm and a will for things to work out to make an impression on Simon. Not every child would fit seamlessly into family life the way she had. Not that it had been easy for her either when her adoptive father had decided he couldn't hack it, but she'd had a special bond with her mother from the first time they'd met and they'd faced all the unexpected obstacles together. At least until she became an adult and decided she should venture out into the big wide world on her own. She wanted that same show of strength they'd had for her to enable her and Simon to work through the aftermath of the school fire but it wasn't going to happen when he kept shutting her out.

Matt shrugged. 'I don't know about that but I've had a lot of practice.'

Quinn nearly choked on her tortilla wrap. 'You have kids of your own?'

It would certainly explain how comfortable he was in that parenting role if there were a load of mini-Matts running around. The lack of wedding ring had blinded her to that possibility. Then again, marriage wasn't always a precursor to fatherhood. He could also be an absentee father but he didn't seem the type to have abandoned little Irish babies around the countryside either.

He spluttered into his glass. 'Hell, no!'

The emphatic denial should've pleased her to know he wasn't a feckless father but it was a stark reminder that the life she'd chosen wasn't for everyone. At least he was upfront about it, unlike Darryl, who'd pretended to be on board with family life and bailed at the last minute.

'You're not going to tell me you actually hate kids or something, are you?' Her heart sank in anticipation of more disappointment. She couldn't bear to find out this affable surgeon had been nothing more than an act. If so, he deserved an Oscar for well and truly duping everyone who knew him from the Castle.

The sound of his deep chuckle buoyed her spirits back up again.

'Not at all. They're grand. As long as I'm not in charge of them outside work.'

'Ah, you're not the settling down type, then?' It

was blatant nosiness but he seemed such perfect husband and father material she couldn't let it pass without comment. Not that she was actively looking for either when it hadn't worked out so well the first time around. She'd clearly been out of the dating scene too long since she was sitting here thinking about playing happy families with the first man to show her any attention.

'I've only just been released into the wild again. My dad died a while back, when I was in medical school. Cancer. I was left to raise my three sisters on my own. Bridget, the youngest, enrolled in college last year and moved away so I feel as though I'm finally starting my adult life. Child free.' He took a short break from devouring his dinner, the subject interfering with his appetite too.

Both she and Matt's siblings had been lucky they'd had someone special who'd been willing to sacrifice everything to provide for them. She wanted to do the same for Simon if he'd only let her.

'That must've been tough.' She was barely coping with one small boy and a part-time job. It was almost incomprehensible to imagine a young Matt raising and supporting a family while studying at the same time. Just when she thought this man couldn't be any more perfect his halo shone that bit brighter.

It was a shame that no-kids rule put him firmly off-limits. Along with the whole medical ethics thing and the fact she'd chosen celibacy over trusting a man in her life again. As if she'd ever stand a chance anyway after he'd witnessed her puffy panda eyes and been drenched in her tears of self-pity. He'd probably endured a lot more as a single parent and cried a lot less.

'Do you want some of my chips? Help yourself.' He shoved his plate towards her and it took a second to figure out why he was trying to feed her.

'Er…thanks.' She helped herself to a couple to detract from the fact she'd probably been staring at him longingly.

Better for him to think she was greedy than

love struck. She wasn't too happy about the nature her thoughts had taken recently either.

'It wasn't easy but we survived and you will too. You figure this stuff out as you go along.'

It was good of him to share some of his personal details with her—he didn't have to and she knew he'd only done it to make her feel better. It did. He was no longer an anonymous authority figure; he was human and he was opening up to her. A little knowledge of his private life made it easier to trust another kindred spirit. She supposed it was only fair she gave something of herself too, although he'd probably already heard more than enough about her for one day.

'I thought with my background this would all be familiar territory. I was a foster kid myself. My birth parents were too young to handle parenthood and I bumped around the system until I was finally adopted. My mum never seemed to struggle the way I have, even when her husband walked out. I'm afraid history repeated itself. My ex left me too when I decided I wanted to foster.'

It was difficult not to take it personally that any

important male figures in her life had abandoned her. From the emotional outbursts and irrational behaviour Matt had probably already figured out why no man wanted to face a future with her.

'We're all full of good intentions, but it's not long before a cold dose of reality soon hits home, eh?' He was smiling at her but Quinn was convinced there was a barbed comment in there. Perhaps he'd meant well by asking her to meet here but he'd found it tougher going than he'd imagined listening to her whining.

'I'm sorry. I shouldn't be lumbering you with all my problems. It's not part of your job description and I'm putting you off your food.'

'Not at all.' He wedged the last bit of his burger into his mouth to prove her wrong.

'I tutor from home so it's been a while since I've had any adult company to vent with. Lucky you, you get to hear me offload first.'

'It's a hazard of the job. I'm a surgeon-cum-counsellor.' His grin said he didn't mind at all.

It was a relief to get off her chest how much these past two months had impacted on her and not be judged on it. She was doing enough of that herself by constantly comparing herself to her mother when the circumstances were so different. She'd been a young girl in the country, desperate for a family, and Simon, well, he wasn't more than a baby and had already been through so much. He'd been passed around like an unwanted guest and now he was burned and traumatised by the fire, with no real idea of what was going to come of him.

Her mother had had an advantage simply by living in her rural surroundings. Fresh air and wide open spaces were more conducive to recovery and peace of mind than the smog and noise of the city. However, this was the best place for him to be for his treatment and there was no choice but to soldier on, regardless of location.

'Do you have a couch in your office we can share?' It wasn't until he raised his eyebrow in response she realised how inappropriate that sounded. Today, it was becoming a habit.

An image of more inappropriateness on the furniture behind closed doors with Matt filled her head and made her hot under her black tank top and slouchy grey cardigan. If she'd had any intention of flirting she definitely would've picked something more attractive than her slummy mummy attire. Comfy leggings and baggy tops were her security blanket inside the hospital and hadn't been meant for public display.

'I mean...I feel as though I should be lying on your couch...you taking notes. As a counsellor, obviously. Not some sort of sofa fetishist who gets off on that sort of thing. I'll shut up now before you do actually use your authority to call the men in white coats to lock me up.' Quinn clapped her hands over her face as if they provided some sort of invisibility shield for her mortification. Unfortunately, they weren't a sound barrier either as she heard Matt cough away his embarrassment.

Very smooth. Not.

Far from building the beginnings of a support system with Matt as a friend, she'd created an even bigger chasm between them with her weirdness. She'd made it crystal clear to herself, and

Matt, through her awkward small talk and vivid imagination that she fancied the pants off him. Why else would she be stumbling over her words and blushing like a schoolgirl trying to make conversation with him.

Great. On top of everything else she was actually picturing him with his pants fancied all the way off! The poor man had no clue about the monster he'd created by being so nice to her.

A sweaty, red-faced monster who'd apparently woken up from hibernation looking for a mate.

CHAPTER FOUR

FOR A SECOND Matt thought he was going to need someone to perform the Heimlich manoeuvre on him to dislodge the French fry in his throat. The shock of Quinn's imagery had made him swallow it whole.

He gulped down a mouthful of water, relief flooding through him as it cleared his blocked airway.

She hadn't tried to choke him to death on purpose. There'd been absolutely no malice or deliberate attempt on his life as far as he could tell, when Quinn emanated nothing but innocence and the scarlet tint of embarrassment. Neither, he suspected, had she meant to flirt with him but his body had responded all the same to the idea of them rolling around in his office. Around this woman he lost all control of himself, body and mind. Not to mention his common sense.

His first mistake had been to come here outside of work, only to be compounded by swapping details of their personal lives. Then there was the touching. Offering a reassuring hand, or shoulder to cry on, was part and parcel of his job, but probably not when they were lost in each other's eyes in a crowded pub.

She drew that protective nature of his to the fore when he'd spent this past year trying to keep it at bay. He'd only intended to show her she wasn't alone because he knew how it was not to have anyone to turn to when you were weighed down with family stresses. She didn't have to apologise for the feisty spirit she'd shown as they clashed over Simon's treatment; she'd need it to get her through. He simply hadn't expected that spark of attraction to flare to life between them as if someone had flicked a switch.

It had thrown him, sent him scurrying to the bar to wait until it passed. Quinn was the mother of one of his patients.

A mother. His patient.

Two very good reasons to bypass that particular circuit, but no, he kept on supplying power.

Telling her about his family was an eejit move. That was personal and this wasn't supposed to be about him. He listened, he diagnosed and he operated but he never, ever got personally involved. Not only had he given something of himself by revealing his family circumstances, now he knew her background too. The fact she'd been through the foster system only made her strength all the more remarkable to him.

She was a true survivor and yet she was still willing to give so much of herself to others. He needed to direct her somewhere those qualities weren't a personal threat to his equilibrium.

'You know, if you're at a loss for company, I can introduce you to members of the hospital committee. I'm sure you've heard the board is trying to close the place down and we'd be only too glad to have someone else fighting in our corner.' It would give her something to focus on other than Simon's treatment and, in turn, might create a bit of distance between them too. She might make a few more friends into the bargain. Friends who weren't afraid to get too close to her in case it compromised their position or freedom.

'I did do a spot of picketing today. It would be such a shame to see the place close. Especially after everything you've done for Simon there. What happens to you if they do close? What happens to us?'

He could see the absolute terror in her eyes, that brilliant blue darkening to the colour of storm-filled skies, at the thought of more disruption in their lives. It was also an indication that she was relying on him being present in her life for the foreseeable future and that wasn't an expectation he could live up to.

'I'd hate to see the place get phased out. Hopefully the campaigning and fundraising will make a difference. As for me, I'm on a temporary contract. I'll move on soon enough anyway. Like I said, I prefer to be footloose and fancy free these days.'

'Simon will miss you terribly.' She broke eye contact and diligently tidied the empty plates into a pile for the server to collect.

A dagger jabbed Matt in the heart at the idea that he'd be the one to cause either of them any further distress.

'Don't worry, I'll be around for a while yet and if I stay local there's always a chance he'd get referred to me anyway.' At least by then he would've had a cooling off period from this particular case.

Quinn nodded, although the lip-chewing continued.

This was the first time his casual new lifestyle had given him cause to rethink his idea of moving from one place to another whenever the mood took him. Whilst the notion of experiencing new people and places was more attractive than remaining stagnant in Dublin, he hadn't given any thought to patients who might get too attached, or vice versa.

It would be tough to leave his patients here when the time came, but better for him. He'd spent a huge chunk of his life on hold, waiting until others were ready to let go of him. This was supposed to be *his* time to spread his wings and not get dragged back into any more family dramas.

Despite the hustle and bustle of the pub around them, he and Quinn fell into an uneasy silence. His attraction to her was in direct competition with his longing for a quiet, uncomplicated life. The two weren't compatible, and whichever won through, it would undoubtedly leave the bitter taste of loss behind.

The vibration in his pocket shocked him back into the present, his pager becoming a cattle prod to make sure he was back on the right path. Although the message informing him Simon was awake had come too late to save him from himself or from straying onto forbidden territory.

'Simon's awake. We should head back.' And put a stop to whatever this is right now.

Quinn's face lit up at the news, which really wasn't helping with the whole neutral, platonic, not-thinking-of-her-as-anything-other-than-a-parent stance he was going to have to take.

'Oh, good! What are we waiting for?'

There was genuine joy moving in to chase the clouds of despair away in those eyes again. Whether Quinn knew it, or wanted it, Matt could see Simon was the most important thing in her life. He knew fostering was only supposed to be a temporary arrangement until a permanent home for the child was secured and if she wasn't careful with her heart she'd end up getting hurt. If he'd had to, Matt would've fought to the death with the authorities to gain custody over his siblings and he knew he'd have been heartbroken to see them shipped out to strangers after everything he'd done for them.

He didn't know what Quinn's long-term plans were, but it was important she didn't lose sight of her own needs or identity in the midst of it all. At least he'd had his career to focus on when his family had flown the nest and stripped him of his parent role.

Quinn was the sort of woman who needed to be cared for as well as being the nurturer of others.

He didn't know why he felt the need to be part of that.

The good news that Simon was awake was a welcome interruption for Quinn. She wasn't proud of the display she'd put on today and it would be best if she and Simon could just disappear back to the house and take her shame with her. At least she could unleash her emotions there without sucking innocent bystanders into the eye of the storm along with her.

Poor Matt, whose only job was to operate on Simon and send them on their way, had run the gauntlet with her today. Irrational jealousy, fear, rage, self-pity and physical attraction—she'd failed to hide any of them in his presence. That last one in particular gave her the shame shudders. He'd been antsy with her ever since that sofa comment.

That sudden urge to crumple into a melting puddle of embarrassment hit again and she wrapped her cardigan around her body, wishing it had a hood to hide her altogether.

She wasn't stupid. That suggestion she should join the hospital committee was his subtle way of getting her to back off and go bother someone else. He'd made his position very clear—he was done with other people's kids unless it was in the operating theatre.

'Are you cold?' Matt broke through her woolly invisibility shield with another blast of concern. He was such a nice guy, it was easy to misinterpret his good manners for romantic interest and that's exactly what she'd done.

If she asked around she'd probably find a long line of lonely, frightened women who were holding a candle for him because of his bedside manner. One thing was sure, when he did move on he'd leave a trail of broken hearts behind him.

'Yeah.' She shivered more at the thought of Matt leaving than the sudden dip in temperature as they ventured outside. He'd become a very big part of their lives here and she couldn't imagine going through all of this without him.

Warmth returned to her chilled bones in a flash as perfect gentleman Matt draped his jacket around her shoulders. In another world this would have been a romantic end to their evening and not a doctor's instinct to prevent her from adding hypothermia to her list of problems. She should have declined the gesture, insisted it wasn't necessary when they'd soon be back indoors, to prevent her from appearing any more pathetic than she already did. Except the enveloping cocoon of his sports coat was a comfort she needed right now. It held that spicy scent she associated with his usually calming presence in its very fabric.

She supposed it would be weird if she accidentally on purpose forgot to return it and started wearing it as a second skin, like some sort of obsessed fan.

When they reached the hospital lobby she had no option but to extricate herself from the pseudo-Matt-hug. If she didn't make the break now there was every likelihood she'd end up curled up in bed tonight using it as a security blanket.

'Thanks. That'll teach me for leaving home

without a coat. Mum would not be happy after all those years of lecturing me about catching my death without one.' Although she'd be tempted to do it again for a quick Matt fix if she thought she could achieve it without the cringeworthy crying it had taken to get one.

He helped her out of his jacket and shrugged it on over his broad shoulders.

Yeah, it looked better on him anyway.

Given their difference in height and build she'd probably looked even more of a waif trailing along behind him. So not the image any woman wanted to give a man she was attracted to. If she was to imagine Matt's idea of a perfect partner it would be one of those oh-so-glamorous female managers who seemed to run the departments here, with their perfect hair and make-up looking terribly efficient. Nothing akin to a messy ponytail, and a quick swipe of lipgloss on a bag lady who didn't know if she was coming or going most of the time. Any romantic notion she held about Matt needed to be left outside the doors of this elevator.

'You don't have to go up with me. I know this place like the back of my hand. Thanks for your help today but I can take it from here. We'll see you again at our next appointment.' She jabbed the button to take her back to Simon, trying not to think about who, or what, Matt had planned for the rest of the night without her.

'I'm sure you can but I promised Simon I'd come and see him. Remember? I wouldn't want to renege on our deal.' Matt stepped into the lift behind her.

It wasn't unexpected given his inherent chivalry but as the steel doors closed, trapping them in the small space together, Quinn almost wished he had gone back on his word so she could breathe again. In here there were no other distractions, no escape from the gravitational pull of Matt McGrory.

She tried not to make eye contact, and instead hummed tunelessly rather than attempt small talk, meaning that the crackling tension remained until another couple joined them on the next floor. Extra bodies should've diffused her urge to throw

herself at him and give in to the temptation of
one tiny kiss to test her theory about his hidden
passion, but the influx only pushed them closer
together until they were touching. There was no
actual skin-to-skin contact through the layers of
their clothes but the static hairs on the back of
her neck said they might as well be naked.

Another heavyset man shoulder-barged his way
in, knocking Matt off balance next to her.

'Sorry,' he said, his hand sliding around her
waist as he steadied himself.

Quinn hoped her cardi wasn't flammable because she was about to go up like a bonfire.

His solid frame surrounded her, shielding her
from any bumps or knocks from the growing
crowd. He had a firm grip on her, protecting her,
claiming her. She thought it was wishful thinking on her part until they arrived at their floor
and he escorted her out, refusing to relinquish
his hold until they were far from the crowd. His
lingering touch even now in the empty corridor
was blowing her he's-only-being-polite theory
out of the water. Surely his patience would've

run out by now if all of this had simply been him humouring her?

It was a shame he hadn't come into her life before it had become so complicated, or later, when things were a bit more stable. Pre-Darryl, when she hadn't been afraid to let someone get close, or post-Simon, when she might have some more control over what happened in her life.

He'd made it clear he wasn't interested in a long-term relationship with anyone but she didn't want to close the door on the idea altogether. Men like Matt didn't come around very often and someday she knew she'd come to regret not acting on this moment. Perhaps if one of them actually acknowledged there was more going on between them other than Simon's welfare she might stand a chance of something happening.

'Matt, I think we should talk—'

Before she could plant the seed for a future romantic interlude, Matt sprang away from her *à la* scalded cat. She barely had time to mourn the loss of his warmth around her when she spotted the reason for the abrupt separation.

'Hey, Rebecca.'

Another member of staff headed towards them. A woman whose curves were apparent even in her shapeless scrubs. The rising colour in Matt's cheeks would've been endearing if it wasn't for the fact Quinn was clearly the source of his sudden embarrassment.

'Hi, Matt. What on earth are you still doing here? Weren't you supposed to be going somewhere tonight?' A pair of curious brown eyes lit on Quinn and she immediately realised how selfish she'd been for monopolising his time. It hadn't entered her head that he would've given up a glamorous night out to sit listening to her tales of woe in a dingy pub.

Matt slid his green-eyed gaze at her too, and Quinn hovered between the couple, very much an outsider in the conversation. There was clearly something unsaid flying across the top of her head. Metaphorically speaking, of course. She had the advantage of a couple of inches in height on the raven-haired doctor. But it was the only one she had here, as she didn't know what they were talking about, or indeed, what relationship they might have beyond being work colleagues. It wasn't any of her business, yet she had to refrain from rugby-tackling the pretty doctor to the ground and demanding to know what interest she had in Matt.

Okay, so she was a little more invested in Matt than she'd intended.

'I...er...changed my mind. I wanted to check in on one of my patients, Simon, one of the kids from the school fire. This is his mum, Quinn. Quinn, this is Rebecca Scott, a transplant surgeon here at the Castle.'

Finally, she was introduced into the conversation before she started a catfight over a man who wasn't even hers.

'I'm so sorry you were caught up in that. I know it's been horrendous for all involved but I hear Simon's treatment's going well?' Rebecca reached out in sympathy and dampened down any wicked thoughts Quinn might've harboured towards her.

'It is. In fact, I'm just going to see him now after his surgery.'

'Well, he's definitely in the best hands.' There was admiration there but Quinn didn't detect anything other than professional courtesy.

'Yes, he is. Listen, Matt, I'm going to go and see how he is. I'll catch up with you later. Nice to meet you, Rebecca.' She didn't hang around for Matt's inevitable insistence he accompany her, nor did she look back to overanalyse the couple's body language once she'd left. They had separate lives, different roles in Simon's future, which didn't necessarily equate to a relationship or a debt to each other. She was confusing her needs with his and a clear head was vital in facing the months ahead. It was down to her to prepare Simon for his future family and she couldn't do that whilst pining for one of her own. Until then, she'd do well to remember it was just the two of them.

'What are you doing?' Rebecca moved in front of Matt, blocking his view of Quinn walking away.

'Hmm?' He was itching to follow her so they could see Simon together but the manner in which she'd left said she didn't want an audience for the reunion. She could be emotional at the best of times and seeing her five-year-old post-surgery would certainly give her cause for more tears. He'd give her a few minutes' privacy before he joined them, and as soon as he'd fulfilled his promise to the boy, he'd do what he should've done in the first place and go home.

Quinn rounded the corner and vanished from sight. It had been a long day for all of them and he didn't want to abandon her when she was so fragile. Instead, he turned his attention back to Rebecca to find her with her arms folded, eyebrows raised and her lips tilted into a half-smile.

'I told Simon I'd show him how to do a few magic tricks before he went home. I thought cheering him up was more important than a few drinks with someone I hardly know.'

'I believe you,' she said, her voice dripping with enough sarcasm to force Matt to defend his presence here post-shift.

'What? You think there's something going on with me and Quinn? She's having a nightmare of a time with Simon and he seems to respond better when I'm around. That's all.' He shut down any gossip fodder without the utterance of a lie. Anything remotely salacious resided entirely in his head. For now.

'Uh-huh? It's not like you to turn down a hot date for a charity case.' Rebecca wasn't about to let this drop and he knew why when he'd been enthusing about the date he'd lined up all week, only to have blown it off at the last minute. It was no wonder he'd developed something of a reputation due to his reluctance to settle down with one woman.

It was true; there'd been a few female interests over the course of his time in London but that didn't mean he jumped into bed with a different partner every week. Sometimes he simply enjoyed a little company. However, the slight against his character was nothing to the umbrage he took to Quinn being denigrated to a pity date. After two months of sparring and making up, he'd go as far as to say that they'd bonded as friends.

He pursed his lips together so he wouldn't defend her honour and give Rebecca any more ammunition to tease, or admonish, him.

'You know me, I'm never short of female company.' Generally he wasn't big-headed about such matters but it was better to shrug it off as a non-event than turn it into a big deal. The girl he was supposed to be seeing tonight, Kelly—or was it Kerry?—was just someone he'd met the other day. It was nothing special and neither of them had been particularly put out when he'd phoned to call it off so he could meet with Quinn instead. He wasn't a player and it wasn't as if he was trying to keep his options open. There was a good chance he'd never see or speak to Kelly/Kerry again.

'No, but it is quite uncharacteristic of you to be so...hands on, at work.'

So she'd seen him with his arm around Quinn. He couldn't even defend his actions there. There'd been no excuse for him to maintain that close contact after they'd exited the packed lift except for his own pleasure. He'd enjoyed the warmth of her pressed into him, her petite frame so delicate against his bulk and the scent of her freshly washed hair filling his nostrils until he didn't want anything else to fill his lungs.

'Simon's a special boy. He's in foster care and I guess I do have a soft spot for him. He's one of the first patients I've been able to treat with spray-on skin, so I'm particularly interested in his progress for use in other cases.' He didn't delve into any other personal aspects of his affinity for the pair. Rebecca knew he had younger sisters, but as this was his new start, he hadn't seen the need to divulge his personal struggles to reach this point. As far as anyone needed to know, he was simply escorting an anxious mother back to her son post-surgery.

'It's easy to get attached. I guess I was hoping for some juicy gossip to take my mind off things.'

'Well, I'm not the one everyone's talking about around here. The rumour mill's gone into overdrive now Thomas is back.'

Rebecca's sigh echoed along the corridor at the mention of her ex-husband. It might have come across as a dirty trick to shift focus from one taboo subject to another but he was genuinely concerned for his friend too. By all accounts the end of her marriage had been traumatic. The car crash which had claimed the life of her young daughter had also proved too much for the marriage to survive. Now her ex, a cardiologist, was here on loan, it was bound to be awkward for both of them.

Matt had seen grief rip apart many families in his line of work and in that respect he was lucky to have kept his own together. The alternative didn't bear thinking about.

'Me and Thomas? There's no story to tell, I assure you. In fact, we haven't exchanged a word since he got here. You'd never believe we knew each other, never mind that we were married once upon a time.' Her smile faltered as she was forced to confront what were obviously unresolved issues with her ex.

'How long has it been since you saw him last?'

'Five years, but in some ways it feels like only yesterday.' The hiccup in her voice exposed the raw grief still lingering beneath the surface.

'I'm sure it's not easy. For either of you.' They'd both lost a child and it was important to remember they'd both been affected. He didn't know Thomas but he knew Rebecca and she wouldn't have given her heart away to someone who wasn't worthy of her.

'It's brought a lot of memories back, good and bad. At some point I think we do need to have an honest conversation about what happened to clear the air, something we never managed when we were still together. Perhaps then we might both get some closure.'

Given that they were going to be working together, they'd need it. According to the staff who'd seen them together, the tension was palpable, and it wasn't like Rebecca not to speak her mind. As she'd just proved with this ambush. Thank goodness she hadn't spotted them getting cosy in the pub or he'd really have had a job trying to explain himself.

'I hope you sort things out. Life's too short to stay mad.'

'We'll see. When all is said and done this isn't about us. We're only here to do our jobs.' On cue, her pager went off and put an end to their impromptu heart-to-heart. She shrugged an apology as she pushed the call button for the elevator.

'I'm sure it'll all work out in the end.'

Rebecca was a professional, the best in her field, and there was no way she'd let personal matters interfere with her patients' welfare. That was one of the golden rules here and one he'd do well to remember himself.

'We've all got to face our demons at some time, I guess. Right, duty calls. Stay out of trouble.'

If he was going to do that, he wouldn't be heading to Simon's room, straight towards it.

CHAPTER FIVE

ALTHOUGH SEEING SIMON had come through the surgery successfully was always a relief, his aftercare never got any easier. Each stage of the treatment was often punctuated with a decline in his behaviour once they left the hospital grounds. From the moment he opened his eyes it was as if they'd taken two steps backwards instead of forward.

She'd stroked his hair, told him what a brave boy he was, promised him treats—all without the normal enthusiastic response of a child his age in return. Of course, they'd see the psychologists, who would do their best to get him to open up and help him work through the trauma, but the onus was still on her to get him past this. With a degree in child psychology herself, she really thought she'd make more progress with him. At least get him to look at her. She'd aced her written exams but the practical was killing her. Most kids would only be too glad to get out of here and go home—she knew she would be—but no amount of coaxing could get him to even acknowledge her.

When Matt strolled into the room and instantly commanded his attention she had to move away from any items which could suddenly become airborne. Although, after their dinner chat, she was able to watch their interaction through new eyes.

He'd had more experience in parenthood than her, his ease very apparent as he engaged Simon in his magic know-how. Perhaps that's what made the difference. He was comfortable around children, whereas she'd had virtually no experience other than once being a child herself. Even then, she hadn't socialised a great deal. Her mother had worked hard to keep a roof over their heads and often that meant missing out on playdates and birthday parties to help her at her cleaning jobs.

It could be that Simon's unease was in direct

correlation to hers and he was picking up on the what-the-hell-am-I-doing? vibes. In which case his lack of confidence in her was understandable. Unfortunately, the fostering classes she'd attended hadn't fully equipped her to do the job. Unlike star pupil Matt, who was deep in conversation sitting on the end of Simon's bed.

'What's with all of the whispering going on over there?' She dared break up the cosy scene in an attempt to wedge herself in the middle of it.

There was more whispering, followed by a childish giggle. A sound she thought she'd never hear coming from Simon and one which threatened to start her blubbing again. She was tempted to throw a blanket over Matt's head and snatch him home with her to keep Simon entertained.

'Can't tell you. It's a secret.' Simon giggled again, his eyes bright in the midst of the dressings covering his face.

'Magician's code, I'm afraid. We can't divulge our secrets to civilians outside our secret circle.' Matt tapped the side of his nose and Simon slapped his hand over his mouth, clearly enjoying the game.

Quinn didn't care as long as he was talking again and having fun.

'Hmm. As long as we're not suddenly overrun with rabbits pulled out of hats, then I'll just have to put up with it. Tell me, what do you have to do to be part of this prestigious group anyway?' She perched on the bed beside Matt, getting a boost from sitting so close to him as much as from the easy-going atmosphere which had been lacking between her and Simon.

'We're a pretty new club so we'll have to look into the rules and regulations. What do you say, Simon? What would it cost Quinn to join?' Matt's teasing was light relief now her green-eyed, monstrous alter ego had left the building. This wasn't about one-upmanship; he was gaining Simon's confidence and trust and gradually easing her in with him.

'Chocolate ice cream!' he shouted without hesitation.

'We can do that.' She was partial to it herself

and something they could easily pick up on the way home. A small price to pay for a quiet night.

'That should cover her joining fee…anything else?' Matt wasn't going to let her off so easily.

'Umm…' Simon took his time, milking her sympathy for all it was worth with Matt's encouragement.

He eventually came back with 'The zoo!' knowing he had her over a barrel.

There was no way she could say no when they were making solid progress. Not that she was against the idea; it simply hadn't crossed her mind that he would want to go.

'Nice one.' Matt high-fived his mini-conspirator and Quinn got the impression she'd walked straight into a trap.

'A day at the zoo? I've never been myself, but if that's the price I have to pay to join your club I'm in.' It was worth it. He hadn't expressed a desire to leave the house since the fire, unwilling to leave the shadows and venture out into the public domain, so this was a major breakthrough.

It could also turn out to be an unmitigated disaster, depending on how he interacted with other visitors. He'd already endured much staring and pointing from the general public who didn't understand how lucky he was just to survive the injuries, but it was a risk worth taking. If things went well it could bring them closer as well as give him a confidence boost.

'You've never been to the zoo?' Matt was still staring at her over that particular revelation.

'We never got around to it. Mum was always working weekends and holidays to pay the bills and I tagged along with her.' It wasn't anyone's fault; spending time together had simply been more important than expensive days out.

'You don't know what you're missing. Lions, penguins, gorillas…they're all amazing up close.'

She couldn't tell who was more excited, both big kids bouncing at the idea. Although she was loath to admit it, there was a fizz in her veins about sharing the experience with Simon for the first time too. As if somehow she could recapture her childhood and help him reconnect with his at the same time.

'Matt has to come too!' Simon tried to wedge it into the terms and conditions of the deal but he was pushing his luck now.

'I've been before. This is something for you and your mum to do together.' Matt turned and mouthed an apology to her and the penny dropped that he'd been trying to broker this deal for her benefit alone.

'Matt has lots of other patients to treat and he'd never get any work done if he had to keep taking them all to the zoo whenever they demanded it. We'll go, just the two of us, and make a day of it.' Quinn could already sense him shrinking back into his shell. Negotiating with an infant was a bit like trying to juggle jelly—impossible and very messy.

'You can take loads of photos and show me the next time you're here.'

Bless him, Matt was doing his best to keep his spirits up but the spark in Simon had definitely gone out now he knew his favourite surgeon wasn't involved. She knew the feeling.

'Right, mister, it's getting late. We need to get

you dressed and take you home.' Any further arguments or tantrums could continue there, out of Matt's earshot. She wouldn't be surprised to find out he'd taken extended leave the next time they were due back to see him.

'I don't have a home!' Simon yelled, and single-handedly pulled the sheet up over his head, his body shaking under the covers as he sobbed.

Quinn genuinely didn't know what to do; her own heart shattered into a million pieces at his outburst. He didn't count her as his mum, didn't even think of her house as a place of safety, despite everything she'd tried to do for him.

She was too numb to cry and stood open-mouthed, staring at Matt, willing him to tell her what to do next. It wasn't as if she could leave him here until he calmed down; he was her foster child, her responsibility, and it was down to her to provide a home he'd rather be in instead of here.

The foster authorities would certainly form that opinion and it was soul-crushing to learn he'd take a hospital bed on a noisy ward over the boy-friendly bedroom she'd painstakingly decorated in anticipation of his arrival.

She'd been happy to have one parent—why couldn't he?

'You're being daft now. I know for a fact you and Quinn live in the same house. I bet you've even got a football-themed room.' As usual Matt was the one to coax him back out of his cotton cocoon.

'I've got space stuff.' Simon sniffed.

'Wow! You're one lucky wee man. I had to share a room with my sisters so it was all flowers and pink mushy stuff when I was growing up.'

'Yuck!'

'Yuck indeed.' Matt gave an exaggerated shud-der at the memory but it gave Quinn a snapshot of his early life, outnumbered by girls.

'Do you wanna come see?' He peeked his head above the cover to witness the fallout of his lat-est demand.

This time Matt turned to her for answers.

They were stuffed.

If she said no, she hadn't a hope of getting Simon home without a struggle and she was too exhausted to face it. A 'yes' meant inviting Matt further into their personal lives and they couldn't keep relying on him to solve their problems. He'd made it clear he didn't want to be part of any family apart from the one he'd already raised. In her head she knew it was asking for trouble but her heart said, 'Yes, yes, yes!' So far, he'd been the one blazing ember of hope in the dark ashes of the fire.

She gave a noncommittal shrug, leaving the final decision with him. It was a cop out on her behalf, but if he wanted out, now was the time to do it. She was putting her faith in him but his hesitation was more comforting than it should've been. At least she wasn't the only one being put on the spot and it proved some things were beyond even his control. His mind wasn't made up one way or the other about getting further entangled in this mess and that had to be more promising than a firm no.

'My apartment isn't too far away…I suppose I

could get my car, drop you two home and take a quick peek at your room…' The confidence had definitely left his voice.

A five-year-old had got the better of both of them.

'I really couldn't ask you to—'

'Cool!' Simon cut off the polite refusal she was trying to make so Matt didn't feel obligated, even though she didn't mean it. Inside, she was happy-dancing with her foster son.

'Well, it would save us a taxi fare.' She folded easily. A ride home would be so much less stress-ful than the Tube or a black cab. As efficient as the London transport system was, it wasn't traumatised-child-friendly. The fewer strangers Simon had to encounter straight after his sur-gery, the better.

'I'll go get the car and meet you out front in about thirty minutes. That should give you plenty of time to get ready.' He bolted from the room as soon as she gave the green light. It was im-possible to tell whether he wanted to put some distance between them as soon as possible, or whether he intended to get the job done before he changed his mind. Whatever his motives, she was eternally grateful.

For the first night in weeks, she wasn't dreading going home.

Matt stopped swearing at himself the moment he clocked the two figures huddled at the hospital entrance waiting for him. He'd been beating himself up about getting roped into this, but seeing them clutching each other's hands like two lost bodies in the fog, he knew he'd done the right thing. He wouldn't have slept if he'd gone home and left Quinn wrestling a clearly agitated child into the back of a taxi. For some reason his presence was enough to diffuse the tension between the two and, as Simon's healthcare provider, it was his duty to ease him back to normality after his surgery. Besides, it was only a lift, something he would do for any of his friends in need.

The only reason he'd hesitated was because he didn't want people like Rebecca, or Quinn, reading too much into it. He really hadn't been able to refuse when he'd had two sets of puppy dog eyes pleading with him to help.

'Nice car.' Quinn eyed his silver convertible with a smile as he pulled up.

'A treat to myself. Although I don't get out in it as often as I'd hoped. Much easier to walk around central London.' It had been his one great extravagance and what might appear to some as a cliché; to him it had been a symbol of his long-awaited independence.

Yet here he was, strapping a small child into the back seat…

'Yeah. This is made for long drives in the country with the top down.' She ran her hand over the car's smooth curves, more impressed than a lot of his friends who thought it was tragic attention-seeking on his part.

'That's the idea.' Except now he had the image of Quinn in the passenger seat, her ash brown hair blowing in the wind, without a care in the world, he wondered if it was time he traded it in for something more practical, more sedate.

* * *

Quinn's modest house was far enough from the hospital to make travel awkward but it had the bonus of peace and quiet. It was the perfect suburban semi for a happy family and the complete opposite of his modern bachelor pad in the heart of the city. He at least had the option of walking to PCH and did most days. Since moving to London he'd fully immersed himself in the chaos around him. Probably because he'd spent most of his years at the beck and call of his siblings, his surroundings dictated by the needs of his dependents. This kind of white picket fence existence represented a prison of sorts to him and he couldn't wait to get back to his alternative, watch-TV-in-my-pants-if-I-want-to lifestyle.

'You can't get much better than a taxi straight to your door.' He pulled the handbrake on with the confidence of a man who knew he'd be leaving again soon. This was the final destination for any feelings or responsibility he felt for Quinn and Simon today. Tomorrow was another day and brought another list of vulnerable patients who would need him.

'I really can't thank you enough, Matt. I wasn't up to another burst of tantrum before we left.' Quinn's slow, deliberate movements as she unbuckled her seat belt showed her weariness and reluctance to go inside.

The stress she was under was relentless—juggling Simon's injuries with the fostering process and her job. All on her own. The two of them could probably do with a break away from it all.

He glanced back at Simon. 'Someone's out for the count now. He shouldn't give you any more trouble.'

'If I can get him up to bed without disturbing him I might actually get a few hours to get some work done. Then I'll be on standby for the rest of the night with pain relief when he needs it.' She was yawning already at the mere mention of the night ahead.

'Make sure you get a couple of hours' sleep too.'

'That's about as much as we're both getting at

the moment.' She gave a hollow laugh. The lack of sleep would definitely account for the short tempers and general crankiness, not to mention the emotional outbursts.

'Why don't you open the door and I'll carry Sleeping Beauty inside for you?'

She was strong and stubborn enough to manage on her own, he was sure—after all, she'd been coping this far on her own—but it didn't seem very gentlemanly to leave her to carry the dead weight of a sleeping child upstairs. If he delivered Simon directly to his bed there was more chance of him getting out of here within the next few minutes. That was his excuse and he was sticking to it.

Quinn opened her mouth as if to argue the point, then thought better of it, going to open the door for them and leaving him to scoop Simon out of the back seat. It was an indication of how weary she was when she gave in so easily.

As Matt carried Simon up the steep staircase to bed, careful not to jar his arm in the process, he knew he'd made the right call. Leaving a tired, petite Quinn to manage this on her own would have been an accident waiting to happen. He'd had enough experience of doing this with baby sisters who'd sat up long past their bedtimes to negotiate the obstacle with ease.

'Which way?' he mouthed to Quinn, who was waiting for them on the landing.

'In here.' She opened one of the doors and switched on the rocket-shaped night light at the side of the small bed.

Matt eased him down onto the covers and let Quinn tuck him in. She was so tenderly brushing his hair from his face and making sure he was comfortable that in that moment an outsider wouldn't have known they were anything other than biological mother and son.

They tried to tiptoe out of the room together but Simon unfurled his foetal position and rolled over.

'Do you like my room, Matt?' he mumbled, half asleep and hardly able to keep his eyes open.

'Yeah, mate. You're one lucky boy.' He could see how much effort Quinn had gone to in order to create the perfect little boy's room. From the glow-in-the-dark stars on the ceiling, to the planet-themed wallpaper, it had been co-ordinated down to the very last detail. The sort of bedroom a young boy sharing a council flat with three sisters could only have dreamed about.

'Now Matt's seen your room he has to go and you need to get some sleep.' Quinn tucked the loosened covers back around him.

'What-about-the-zoo?' he said in one breath as his eyes fluttered shut again.

'We'll do that another day,' she assured him, and tried to back out of the room again.

'Can-Matt-come-too?' He wasn't giving in without a fight.

Quinn's features flickered with renewed panic. This wasn't in the plan but they knew all hell would break loose again if he left and denied this request. Their silence forced Simon's eyes open and Matt had to act fast or get stuck here all night trying to pacify him.

'Sure.' He glanced back at her and shrugged. What choice did he have? With any luck Simon would forget the entire conversation altogether. Especially since the required answer sent him back to sleep with a smile on his face.

This time they made it out of the room unde-tected and Quinn released a whoosh of breath from her lungs as she eased the door behind them.

'I thought we'd never get out of there alive.' She rested her head against the back of the door, all signs of tension leaving her body as her frown lines finally disappeared and a smile played upon her lips. It was a good look on her and one Matt wished he saw more often.

'We're not off the hook yet but hopefully we've stalled the drama for another day.' Preferably when he was far from the crime scene.

'I appreciate you only agreed to the zoo thing to get him to go to sleep. Don't worry, I won't hold you to it.' She was granting him immunity but he remembered something she'd said about people letting her down and he didn't want to be another one to add to her list.

'It's no problem at all. I told you, I love the

zoo.' It just wasn't somewhere he'd visited since his sisters had entered their teenage years. An afternoon escorting the pair around the sights wasn't a big deal; he'd been the chaperone on a few organised hospital trips in his time and this wouldn't be too dissimilar. It would be worth a couple of hours of his free time to see them happy again.

'Thanks for the idea, by the way. I kind of fell apart when he said he didn't have a home to go to.' The crack in her voice was evidence of how much the comment had hurt.

'He's frightened and it's been another tough day for both of you. It's easy to hit out at the ones closest to us. I've lost count of the amount of times my sisters told me they hated me and they couldn't wait to move out. They didn't mean it, and nor does Simon. It's all part of the extras package that comes with parenthood, I'm afraid.'

There'd been plenty of rows over the years as teenagers rebelled and he'd been the authority figure who'd had to rein them in. However, they were still a close family and he was the first person they'd call if they needed help.

'I'd hate to think I was making things worse for him. He seems so unhappy.' The head was down as the burden of guilt took up residence again on her shoulders.

He crouched down before her so she had to look at him. 'Hey, I don't know Simon's background but I do know he's a lucky boy to have you as a foster mother. You're a wonderful woman, Quinn, and don't you forget that.'

She fluttered her eyelashes as she tried to bat away the compliment but he meant every word. The burden she'd taken on with Simon's injuries and her determination to make a loving home for the duration of his time with her took tremendous courage. A strong, fiery soul wrapped up in one pretty package was difficult not to admire.

Now free from the responsibilities of work and away from the stares of co-workers and impressionable youngsters, Matt no longer had anyone to stop him from doing what he'd wanted to do for a long time.

He leaned in and pressed his mouth to hers, stealing the kiss they'd been dodging since their time in the pub. It wasn't his ego make-believing she wanted this too when her lips were parted and waiting for him.

Away from the hospital they were more than an overattentive doctor and an anxious parent. In another time, in different circumstances, he wouldn't have waited a full day before taking her in his arms the way he did now.

He bunched her silky hair in his hands and thought only of driving away the shadows of doubt already trying to creep in and rob him of this moment. The instant passion which flared between them was a culmination of weeks of building tension, fighting the attraction and each other. Every fibre of his being, with the exception of several erogenous zones, said this was a bad idea. She was a single mother and this went against all of his self-imposed rules. This new carefree lifestyle was supposed to mean he went with the flow, free to do whatever he wanted. And in the here and now, Quinn was exactly what he wanted, so he ignored the voice that told him to leave and never look back, and carried on kissing her.

Either Quinn had died and gone to heaven or her exhaustion had conjured up this mega-erotic fantasy because it couldn't possibly be happening. It was beyond comprehension that she was actually making out with her foster son's surgeon in her own house.

The tug at her scalp reminded her it was very real.

Matt took her gasp as an invitation to plunge his tongue deeper into her mouth, stealing what was left of her breath. He was so thorough in his exploration, yet so tender, he confused her senses until she couldn't think beyond his next touch.

His fingers wrapped around her hair, his mouth locked onto hers, his hard body pressed tightly against her—it was too much for her long-neglected libido to process at once. It was as though every one of her forgotten desires had come to life at once, erasing the loneliness of these past man-free months.

Her ex's betrayal had devastated her so much she'd convinced herself romance in her life didn't matter but Matt McGrory had obliterated that theory with one kiss. It most certainly *did* matter when it reminded her she was a hot-blooded woman beneath the layers of foster mum guilt. She'd forgotten how it was to have someone kiss the sensitive skin at her neck and send shock waves of pleasure spiralling through her belly and beyond. In fact, she didn't remember ever swooning the way she was right now.

Today, Matt had successfully operated on Simon, talked sense into her when she'd been virtually hysterical, held her when she'd cried, supported her when she'd fallen apart and carried a sleeping child to his bed. He was perfect. It was a crying shame the timing was abominable.

He slid a hand under her shirt and her nipples immediately tightened in anticipation of his touch. If he ventured any further than her back she doubted she'd be able to think clearly enough to put a stop to this. As enjoyable as the feel of his lips on her fevered skin was, this wasn't about her getting her groove back on. Simon was her priority and she wouldn't do anything to jeopardise that.

Matt was his surgeon and this could lead to all sorts of complications regarding his treatment and the fostering authorities. That wasn't a risk she was willing to take. She wanted to break the cycle of selfish behaviour which had plagued her and Simon to date, and if it kept her heart protected a while longer, all the better.

'I think we should probably call it a day.' She dug deep to find the strength to end the best night she'd had for a long time.

With her hands creating a barrier between their warm bodies, she gave him a feeble push. Her heart wasn't in the rejection but it did stop him in his tracks before he kissed his way to her earlobe and discovered her kill switch. His acquiescence did nothing to ease her conscience or the throbbing need pulsating in her veins.

'You're probably right.' He took a step back,

giving them some space to think about the disaster they'd narrowly averted. Then he was gone.

One nod of the head, a meek half-smile and it was Goodnight, Josephine.

Quinn exhaled a shaky breath as the front door clicked shut.

It had been a close call and, now she knew the number, it was going to be a test of endurance not to put him on speed dial.

CHAPTER SIX

IT HAD BEEN several days since the infamous kiss but Quinn hadn't laid eyes on Matt at all. Quite a feat when she'd spent every waking moment back at the hospital. She thought he'd be there when Simon had his dressings changed, an ordeal in itself. Although it was the nurses who routinely did that job, he usually called in to see how they were. He was definitely avoiding her.

Whilst his noticeable absence had prevented any awkwardness between them after locking lips together, a sense of loss seemed to have engulfed her and Simon as a result. They'd become much too invested in his company and now she had very fond, intimate memories to make her pine for him too.

It had been her decision to stop things before they'd gone any further. Hot kisses and steamy intervals didn't bring any comfort when there was no commitment behind them. Passion didn't mean much to her these days when she'd found out the hard way men used it to hide their true intentions. She'd thought Darryl had loved her because he was so attentive in that department but when it came down to putting a child's needs before his he'd shown how shallow he really was. She wouldn't be duped for a second time into believing a man's interest in her body was anything more than just that. Darryl had nearly broken her spirit altogether with his betrayal, to the point she'd questioned her own judgement about foster care. What was the point if the whole ideal of a happy family was a sham concocted so the male species could satisfy their own selfish needs?

It was meeting Simon which had convinced her she'd taken the right path and she wouldn't be so easily diverted from it again. A handsome face and a kissable mouth weren't enough for her to risk her or Simon's future if she was dumped again and sent spiralling back down into despair. Things were difficult at the moment but she was still soldiering on, wasn't ready to give up the fight. One more knock to her confidence might well change that. No, she'd made the right call and she'd just have to learn to live with it. Regardless of how much she wanted Matt to be the man she'd always thought would be the head of her perfect little family.

Today, to distract herself from the events of that evening, she'd joined the committee fighting to save the Castle. Whilst Simon was busy with his physiotherapist, who was working with him to make sure he maintained the movement in his right arm, she had some time to herself. She chose to spend it putting the world to rights with other committee members over a latte in the canteen. Her position also allowed her to keep watch on the door in case of a glimpse of the elusive Mr McGrory.

'I'm so glad you've joined us, Quinn. It'll really help our cause to have parents of our patients on board, as well as the staff. This is about the children, and showing the board the Castle is an important part of the community, and is more than just a lucrative piece of land.' Victoria Christie sat forward in her chair, fixing Quinn with her intense hazel eyes. She was a paramedic, the head of the committee and apparently very passionate about the cause.

With her buoyant enthusiasm she was the perfect choice for a front woman and Quinn got the impression she would attach herself to the wrecking ball should the dreaded demolition come to fruition.

'I'm only too happy to help. I'll sign a petition, wave a placard, write a personal impact statement…whatever it takes to make a difference. Matt…er… Mr McGrory suggested I join since I spend most of my days here anyway.' Mostly, she suspected, to get her out of his lovely blond hair, but at least it was a more productive way of filling her time than fretting and crying on shoulders of very busy surgeons.

'Matt's very passionate about his work and his patients. He's one of the good guys.' The tall blonde she'd been introduced to at the start of this meeting was Robyn Kelly, head of surgery at the hospital and the committee's PR person.

Quinn shifted her gaze towards the pile of papers on the table outlining their press coverage so far in case her blush gave away her thoughts about that very personal, private moment she'd spent with her colleague at her house.

'He's been very patient with Simon, and me, but we're well on the way to recovery. I hope future patients are as lucky to have him on their side.' She smiled as brightly as her pained cheeks would allow. In truth, she didn't want anyone to get as close as she had been to him but that didn't mean she'd deny another family his expertise.

'That's a really good idea!' Victoria slammed her cup back down on the table, sloshing the contents into the saucer.

'What is?' With one hand Robyn quickly moved the newspaper cuttings out of the path of the tea puddle slowly spreading across the table, and used the other to soak up the mess with a napkin.

She exuded a self-confidence Quinn had once

had, before a runaway boyfriend and being cat-apulted into life as a single foster parent had robbed her of it. With a little time and more ex-perience she hoped she'd soon be able to clear up her own messes as swiftly and efficiently.

Although she'd never regret her decision to leave her full-time teaching position to raise Simon, she did envy both women to a certain degree. They were still career women, free to gossip over coffee without feeling guilty about taking some 'me' time. It was just as well they'd been so welcoming, arranging this meet as soon as she'd expressed an interest in the committee. Otherwise her jealousy might have got the bet-ter of her again.

'Personal impact stories, of course. Perhaps we could collate short statements from patients and their families, past and present. They could give an account of what the hospital has done for them and what it would mean to lose its support.

'That could add a really heartfelt element to the cause...'

'I could make a start with the families of the

other children who were treated after the school fire.' Quinn knew most of them by sight now, if not personally, and they were certainly aware of Simon. Their kids had been discharged from the hospital long ago whilst he and Ryan, who'd suffered the most serious injuries, were still receiving treatment.

This new mission would give her an introduction into a conversation which didn't have to solely revolve around Simon's trauma. She wasn't the one who bore the physical scars but even she was sick of the sympathetic murmuring every time they walked past.

'Fantastic. That would be better coming from you, a concerned parent, rather than a soon-to-be-out-of-work member of staff.' Victoria's smile softened her features and her praise endeared her to Quinn even more.

'We might even get the papers to run a series of them to really hammer home how much a part of the children's recovery the Castle has become. Honest raw emotion versus cold hard cash...I think my contacts at the paper would be only too glad to wage war on some corporate fat cats.' Robyn was furiously scribbling in a reporter's notebook she'd plucked from her handbag.

'Quinn, I'll pass your name on to a few of the patients who want to help. You could be the co-ordinator for this leg of the campaign, if that's not too much trouble?' After draining her cup, Victoria got to her feet and effectively ended the meeting.

'Not at all. I could even make up some questionnaires to hand out if it would make things easier?' Admin she could do, and while paperwork had been the bane of her teaching career it was something positive here. It gave her an identity which wasn't merely that of Quinn, the single mother. She still had one useful function.

'I'll leave the details to you and try to organise a collection point for the completed papers. I'm really glad you've joined us, Quinn.' Another smile of acceptance and a firm handshake to solidify her role on the team.

Robyn, too, was packing up to leave. 'All excellent suggestions. I'll be sure to put your name forward for a medal or something at the next board meeting if we pull this off. In the meantime, I'm going to go make some more phone calls.'

She gave a sharp nod of her head as though to assure Quinn she'd just passed some sort of initiation test before she vanished out the door after Victoria. It seemed she was the only one not in a hurry to get anywhere.

She took her time finishing her latte and the caffeine seemed to have kicked in as she went to collect Simon with a renewed bounce to her step. Her well-received ideas today gave her hope that somewhere down the line she might come up with another brainwave to aid Simon as well as the hospital.

She rounded the corner and stopped dead, the rubber soles of her shoes squealing in protest on the tiled floor as she pulled on the emergency handbrake.

Unless her eyes were deceiving her, Simon and Matt were walking towards her. Panic slammed into her chest that something was wrong; there was also a fluttering in her pulse, followed by irrational fear again...then relief because they were both smiling. And finally, a surge of gratefulness she'd chosen a dress today instead of her jeans and cardi.

So, her wardrobe choices had become decidedly more feminine this week. It was an ego boost; she felt better inside when she knew she looked good on the outside. It held no significance where Matt was concerned. She definitely hadn't been paying more attention to her make-up and clothes in case she ran into him again so she looked her best. That would mean she regretted telling him to leave the other night which wasn't possible. Her primary focus would always be Simon and any other future foster children over men with wanderlust in their bewitching green eyes.

'Hey. Is everything all right?' She managed to keep her voice steady and un-chipmunk-like regardless of her heart pounding a dizzying beat.

All of the thoughts she'd had about him since that night hit her at once as the sight of him reminded her she hadn't exaggerated the effect he had on her. Her lips tingled with the memory of him there, her skin rippled with goose bumps as though his hand still rested upon her and the hairs stood on the back of her neck where he'd kissed her so tenderly.

She supposed it would be really out of order to grab the fire extinguisher off the wall and hose herself down before she forgot where she was and tried to jump Matt's bones.

'I thought I'd call in and see how things were going.' He ruffled Simon's hair, not meeting her eyes.

Did he mean that in a purely professional capacity? Was he checking in to see how she was after their moment of madness, or just Simon? Why was she overanalysing his every word like a neurotic teenager when she was the one who'd called it a night? She'd forfeited her right to be on his watch-list when she'd directed him towards her front door rather than her bedroom door.

And now her imagination was really going into overdrive, along with her heart rate. Any minute now her tachycardia was going to require a hospital stay of her own if she couldn't stop thinking about Matt without his scrubs.

She cleared her throat and refocused. He was wearing clothes. They were in public. He had Simon by the hand. Anything remotely erotic beyond that was in her disturbed mind.

'We're chugging along as usual.' The only disruption to their carefully organised schedule were the distractions she was seeking to stop her obsessing over a certain medic. 'Oh, and I've volunteered my services to the hospital committee.'

'Good. Good. We can use all the help we can get.' Matt rocked forward and back on his toes, displaying the same unease about seeing each other after their last meet.

Yet, he'd come to seek her out. Albeit using Simon as some sort of barrier between them.

'How did you get on today, sweetheart?' It was never fun waiting on the sidelines no matter what the purpose of the visit because there was no telling how his mood would be at the end of these appointments. No child enjoyed sitting still for too long or being poked and prodded by doctors and nurses. Although there was no dragging of heels when he was with Matt. She should really capitalise on that and get him home while there were some happy endorphins going on.

'Okay.' It was probably as good an answer as she could hope for.

'I took the liberty of checking on Simon while I was here. Everything seems to be healing nicely.'

'Yes. Thanks to you and the rest of the staff.' Praise where it was due, Matt was very skilled at what he did and everyone here was working to ensure Simon's scarring would be as minimal as possible.

'And you. Aftercare at home is equally as important.'

Quinn didn't know how to respond to his kind acknowledgement that she'd contributed to his recovery in some small way. So far, she'd only seen the areas in which she'd failed him.

As they ran out of things to say to each other, memories of that kiss hovered unattended between them, the air crackling with unresolved sexual tension.

'Matt says we can go to the zoo tomorrow.' Leave it to Simon to throw her even more off guard with extra last-minute drama.

'I don't think so.' They'd had this conversation so she could prepare him for the disappointment when they ended up going alone, impressing upon him the importance of Matt's job and how he couldn't take time off when small boys demanded it.

She wouldn't expect Matt to keep his word given the circumstances, when he'd either be nursing a bruised ego or breathing a sigh of relief after she'd rebuffed him. Although, strictly speaking, she hadn't rejected his advances; she'd simply declined a further sample of his wares before she became addicted.

Simon's bottom lip dropped, indicating the moment of calm was about to come to an abrupt end.

'If you have other plans I totally understand. I really should have got in touch sooner.' Matt raked his hand over his scalp, mussing his usually neat locks.

Quinn found it oddly comforting to find she wasn't the only one trying to keep her cool.

'No plans.' Certainly none which included spending another day in adult male company because she apparently had trouble containing herself when left alone with one.

'Good. It's a date, then.' Matt's very words, no matter how innocently intended, shattered her fragile composure.

Whatever deal these two had struck this time, there was no going back on it; otherwise Simon would never forgive her for it. She couldn't afford to be the bad guy here.

'Great,' she said, smiling sweetly while glaring daggers at Matt. She didn't understand why he'd insisted on making this happen when it had been made very clear socialising between them wasn't a good idea at all.

Matt strolled towards the designated meeting point for his day out with Quinn and Simon. He never imagined he'd be back playing the stand-in father figure so soon but he couldn't go back on his word to Simon.

Okay, he wasn't being *totally* altruistic; he hadn't been able to stop thinking about Quinn, or that kiss they'd shared, no matter how hard he'd tried to avoid her. In the end he'd resigned himself to see this through, spurred on in part by the glimpses he'd caught of her flitting in and out of the department like a ghost until he hadn't been entirely sure if she was anything but a figment of his overactive imagination.

It was difficult to convince yourself you weren't interested in someone when they were at your place of work every day and driving you to distraction when you knew how it was to hold them, taste them, be with them.

In the cold light of day he should've been relieved when she'd sent him home for a cold shower. After all, he'd had more than enough family duty stuff to last him a lifetime. Instead, he and his dented male pride had brooded, mourned the loss of something which could've been special.

It was seeing Quinn carry on taking care of Simon regardless of her own wants and feelings which had made him see sense in the end. Forget the playboy car and bachelor pad in the city; he was a thirty-five-year-old man, an adult, and Simon was the child who had to come first.

Now he was committed to this he was going to make it a day to remember. One which wouldn't be dictated by hospitals and authorities for Quinn and Simon. If Matt had learned anything about raising younger sisters, it was how to have fun and keep their young minds occupied away from the harsh realities of life.

Quinn had declined his offer of a lift but he hadn't minded since it reduced his responsibilities for the afternoon. It gave the impression he was more of a tour guide today rather than a date, or part of the family, and that suited him fine. As soon as they were back on the train home he was off the clock with a clear conscience and his promise kept.

Little Venice, with its pretty barges and canals, was only a short distance from his apartment and the Tube station. The perfect place to pick up a couple of tourists already waiting on the bridge for him. They were watching the boats below, oblivious to his arrival, and Matt took a moment to drink in the sight.

Quinn, dressed in a daisy-covered strappy yellow sundress and showing off her toned, tanned limbs, was the embodiment of the beautiful sunny morning. Simply stunning. Simon, too, was in his summer wear, every bit as colourful in his red shirt and green shorts. Quinn knelt to slather on sun cream to Simon's exposed skin and plonked a legionnaire-style cap on his head. As per instructions, she wasn't taking any chances of the sun aggravating his already tender skin.

'Look, Quinn. It's Matt!' Simon spotted him over the top of his foster mother's head and was suddenly running at him full pelt.

'Oof!' A five-year-old hug missile knocked out what was left of his breath after seeing Quinn.

'Hi,' she said, brushing her hair from her eyes as he walked towards her.

Matt held out his hand to help her back to her

feet, with Simon still attached one-handed to his waist. 'It's nice to see you too.'

'Sorry, he's very excited.' With a warning to calm down before Matt changed his mind, Quinn untangled the little person from him. The threat wasn't the least bit likely but it did the job.

'Me too.' Matt's grin reflected that of his co-chaperone for the day and sealed a non-verbal agreement that they'd put their indiscretion behind them and start over.

'Where are the animals?' Simon piped up, understandably anxious when he'd been promised monkeys, giraffes and all kinds of exotic new friends, only to find water and barges as far as the eye could see.

It was all part of Matt's plan to build the excitement a while longer and capture Simon's attention for the main event.

'They're at the zoo, which we're going to, but a tourist trip around London isn't complete without taking in a show.' He could see Quinn frowning at him out of the corner of his eye but the surprise was just as much for her.

Simon skipped between the two adults as they walked down towards the red-and-yellow barge covered with a huge stripy canvas top. They must've looked like any other young family from a distance and he was surprisingly comfortable with that thought...as long as it was short-lived. Today all Matt wanted was for Simon to feel comfortable and the beaming faces beside him said the lie was worth telling.

'A puppet show?' Quinn's eyes were wider than those of the other children trooping past them on the gangplank into the quirky theatre barge.

'I've heard the kids love it and it'll get Simon used to being on board before we take a water taxi on up to the zoo.' Apart from being the perfect excuse for him to see it for himself, the dimly lit area would also serve as a gentle icebreaker into the general public. He didn't want Simon to become too overwhelmed by the hordes of people who'd undoubtedly be at the zoo on a day such as this.

'You really do think of everything.'

It was a compliment, not a criticism, but it was

truer than Quinn would ever know. He hadn't left anything to chance, having planned every tiny detail of this trip in those moments he'd lain awake since agreeing to it.

Matt escorted them to their tiered seats looking down on the small stage, away from prying eyes. The one concern he'd had was that Simon might find the small space too claustrophobic. On his initial admission his notes had mentioned he'd been trapped in one of the classrooms and Quinn had mentioned his nightmares regarding his entrapment and not being able to find his way out. He needn't have worried. Simon was as enthralled with the old-fashioned marionettes adorning the walls as any of the other children. Matt was the only one experiencing difficulties with the low ceiling and small walkways and that was purely down to his height.

'I've never seen a real puppet show before.' Quinn leaned in to whisper in the darkness, her thighs touching his on the small bench where they sat, her excitement inadvertently increasing his.

'Well, they say it's recommended for small kids from five to ninety-five and I think we fall right in the middle of that age bracket.' He reached across to whisper back, the soft waves of her hair brushing his cheek, and it was all he could do not to nuzzle closer and breathe in her sweet scent. This was supposed to be a PG-rated show and he didn't want to run the risk of being asked to walk the gangplank of shame because he couldn't control himself around her.

'In that case, we're the perfect audience.' Her eyes glittered in the darkness as she hugged Simon close.

'Perfect.' Matt ignored the rising curtain, mesmerised by Quinn's childlike wonder instead.

Quinn was in her very own fairy tale. So far she and Simon had been enchanted by their favourite childhood tales brought to life by puppets and had a good old singalong to some very familiar nursery rhymes. Simon had really thrown himself into the audience participation, as had Matt.

Perhaps it was the relative safety of dimmed

lighting which brought her boy out of his shell, or maybe he was simply following the exuberance of Matt's tuneless singing, but in that hour no one could tell he was different from any other boisterous child.

Matt had whisked them straight onto another barge when the show ended and they'd trundled along the tranquil waterways towards the zoo. It was the best route they could've taken, so peaceful, and a world away from the crowded streets beyond the green banks.

She'd been on boats before but never the barges. The hand-painted green-and-red beauty they were travelling on transported them to another era, a parallel universe where everything was well in her world.

How was it Matt could take such a simple idea and turn it into something special?

That was the talent which charmed adults as much as the children.

He was sitting with Simon now, spending the journey time pointing out the sights through the tiny side windows. He had a love and knowledge of the world around him that he was keen to share. Then there was that fun side to him as he encouraged his sidekick to wave at passers-by and make silly noises every time they went under a bridge. A distraction, she guessed, from the odd curious stare and a fear of the dark.

It was probably the first time in his young life he had two adults working together to put his needs above their own. She hoped one day he would have this for real even if she wouldn't. There would be a family for Simon someday but she doubted she'd ever find another Matt who'd take her and her planned foster brood on for anything other than an afternoon. She wasn't lucky that way.

Their gentle journey came to an end in a leafy area which still seemed miles from civilisation. As if sensing her confusion, Matt reached his arm across the seat and rested his hand on her shoulder.

'The waterbus tours have their own entrance into the zoo so there's no need for us to join the queues at the main entrance.'

A warmth started in the pit of Quinn's stomach and gradually spread its way through her system and it wasn't purely because they couldn't seem to help themselves from making body contact when and where they could. On this occasion it was Matt's thoughtfulness which had really captured her heart. Something which had been sadly lacking from the people in her and Simon's lives to date. Without making a big deal about it, he'd carefully constructed a tailor-made route into the busy zoo to suit all of a traumatised child's needs.

From the magical puppet theatre, to the tranquil method of transport, and now this, the trouble he'd gone to just so they could arrive at their destination relaxed brought a lump to her throat.

If only she and Simon had had male role models who took such care of others, they mightn't have had the past heartaches they were both still trying to overcome.

They waited until all the other passengers had disembarked before they left their seats, with Quinn hesitant to leave the sweet memories of their journey here to rejoin the masses on the other side of the hill.

'Your sisters are very lucky to have you,' she said as Matt helped her ashore. If he treated his siblings as well as he did his patients and families they would never have been in doubt about being loved, and that was the most important aspect of growing up in any family.

His brow knitted together trying to fathom what to make of her compliment. She had no doubt he'd experienced the same general struggles as she'd had as a single parent, yet the very fact he didn't expect thanks for getting through them spoke volumes. A person didn't become a parent for awards and accolades but to create the best possible start in life for their children. Be it younger siblings or foster children. Simply by doing her best for Simon, Quinn was beginning to see she was already the best mother he'd ever had.

Simon squeezed her hand as they moved through to the main part of the zoo with people as far as the eye could see. She squeezed back, reassuring him she was here whenever he needed her. That was all she could do for as long as he was with her—love him and protect him as well as she could. Someday that might be enough for him.

As more children, and adults who should've known better, turned to stare at the little boy with the scars and burned skin, she held him closer. Matt took up residence on the other side so they created a protective barrier around him. Somehow they'd get through this together.

CHAPTER SEVEN

'Is it still the done thing to go to the zoo? Should I feel guilty about walking freely around here peering in at caged animals?' As excited as she was to be here, she did have a social conscience and the child-versus-adult argument about it in her head was in danger of tainting the experience.

'There are two very different schools of thought but the zoo today is much more than the sideshow attraction it used to be. It's educational and provides a natural environment for the animals. Then there are the conservation projects which are funded through the admission fees...'

'Okay. Okay. I'm sold. I can enjoy the view safe in the knowledge I'm not contributing to any ill treatment.' She trusted Matt's judgement. He'd done his homework and he wasn't the sort of man to throw his weight behind a cause unless it was for the greater good. He was principled and not the type to bend the facts to suit his own agenda. Unlike her ex, who'd pretended he wanted a family so he could move in with her.

Quinn shooed away the negative thoughts from her past to replace them with the positive. Such as Matt, positively yummy in his casual clothes again this morning. As he turned to study the map, she was free to ogle his backside encased in black denim and the perfect V of his torso wrapped in dark grey cotton.

'What are you smiling at, Quinn?' Simon quizzed, drawing Matt's attention back from the map.

Caught in the act of perving at Matt's physical attributes, lies didn't come easy to her. 'I, er...I was just thinking nice thoughts.'

She spun on her heel and started walking again, ignoring the smirk on Matt's face and the heat of her own.

'What ones?' Simon tugged her hand with

the unfiltered curiosity only a child could get away with.

The puppets. The boat. Matt's butt.

She could've said any of those things and they would've been true.

In the end she went with, 'About how much fun I'm having with you both today.'

Curiosity satisfied, Simon moved on to his new topic of interest, staring at the pictures of ice creams depicted on an advertising board.

'Can I have one?'

'It's a bit early for ice cream but we can get one later. All good boys and girls deserve a treat now and then, don't you think, Quinn?' Matt was so close his breath tickled the inside of her ear and did something to her that made her a very bad girl.

She so wanted him to be talking about more than a child or an ice cream.

Up until now she'd been the very model of restraint but she was wondering if she deserved a treat too? They did say a little of what you fancy was good for you and there was no denying what it was she fancied more than anything.

'Absolutely. Life can get very dull if you don't give in to temptation once in a while.' She locked eyes with Matt so that all pretence they were still talking about dairy products vanished without trace.

Eye contact definitely constituted flirting when the heat flaring between them was hotter than the morning sun. They'd proved they could be adults, and whatever did or didn't happen between them personally wouldn't become an issue where Simon was concerned. There was no fostering law against her seeing someone either, except the one she'd created herself. By trying to protect her heart she might actually be denying herself the best thing that had walked into her life since Simon.

Despite the unexpected trials and tribulations which had made their journey more difficult than it should've been, she couldn't imagine her existence without Simon in it. Or Matt, for that matter, and therein lay the danger. The damage had already been done, because she knew when the time came for these two to leave, all she'd have left would be a broken heart and some wonderful memories.

Today was all about making those memorable moments and as long as they avoided any empty promises they might actually get to make a few. Matt was a boost to her confidence when he did his best to convince her she could handle whatever fate threw at her. That was every bit as enticing as the soft lips which had caressed hers and the warm hands she could still imagine on her skin. He was right. She did deserve a treat.

Away from impressionable young eyes who might read more into an adult relationship than was true, she wanted one more taste of her dishy doc.

They made their way around the exhibits, each animal becoming Simon's new favourite as he was introduced to their habitats, and eventually circled back to the area where they'd started. Their route had been dictated according to which animals Simon wanted to see rather than the logical, more traditional route everyone else was following. It had probably added a few extra miles to their journey but that could be to their advantage later when exhaustion caught up with him.

Quinn had to admit a pang of self-pity for her inner child when she was only getting to experience this herself at the age of thirty-two. Watching Simon's face light up every time a penguin swam close or a monkey swung by, she ached for the little girl who'd been denied this joy with her own parents.

Every child should experience the fun and wonder to be had in the world beyond school and the foster system and she vowed to do it for whoever entered her care. It didn't have to be the zoo, or with Matt, but she wanted her future foster children to have at least one day of simply being a kid.

'You wish you could get in there, don't you?'

'Sorry?' Quinn panicked that Matt had caught her ogling his backside again.

'The meerkat tunnels. I can see you're busting

to get in those with him.' He nodded over towards Simon, who'd popped his head up in the plastic capsule overlooking the enclosure.

'Yeah. This place is great, so interactive for the kids, but us adults might want to find out what it's like to be a meerkat for the afternoon too.' She covered herself quickly, happy to acknowledge her play envy before her relationship daydreams. After all, she didn't know if Matt saw her as anything other than an acquaintance now. He'd certainly been in control of any more urges to kiss her. More's the pity.

Despite the flirting and the unnecessary touching, which she could have misconstrued entirely, he hadn't made another move on her.

'Poor Quinn. I hear they do some adult-only tours of the zoo at night. Perhaps we should sign up for one?' He was teasing her but he painted an enticing picture of an intimate party of two having some fun together at night.

'It seems to me that we both missed out on the whole childhood fun thing. It mightn't be a bad idea for us to have some quality time in the dark.'

Her temperature rose with the bold proposal, as did Matt's eyebrows.

'Hold that thought,' he growled into her ear as Simon came running back to greet them.

'When are we getting something to eat?'

'Soon.' She was glad he was getting his appetite back and she would simply have to set aside her hunger for anything other than lunch until she and Matt were alone again.

Matt thought he'd imagined the heat shimmering between them, a manifestation of his own frustration that he and Quinn hadn't progressed to anything beyond that one sizzling kiss. He'd wanted more but when she'd given him his marching orders he'd done his best to ignore the temptation. That was until he'd seen the darkening of her eyes, the sapphire fire matching the one burning inside him.

He wasn't a man to disappoint anyone if he could help it but there was a time and place for everything and at this very moment they had a hungry boy to feed.

He'd arranged a special child-sized lunch for

them. Although the restaurant was crowded with most tables and chairs occupied, they were able to slip into a quiet side room where they served a more civilised afternoon tea.

'This is amazing! You're really spoiling us today.' Quinn clapped her hands together as the arrangement of mini-rolls, sandwiches and bite-sized cakes and scones arrived, presented on a small picnic bench.

'You're worth it,' he said, hoping he sounded more complimentary than cheesy.

He meant it. She should have someone treating her every day and making her feel special. The delight on her face and her grateful smile puffed Matt's chest out that he'd been the one to put it there and he didn't want anyone else to have the privilege.

When he'd planned this day he'd convinced himself he'd be glad when it was over, his responsibility to the pair outside the hospital over for good. Now that they were coming to the last stages, he was beginning to have second thoughts. He could honestly say this was one of the best days he'd had since moving to London and that was entirely down to the company. It would be stupid to end things here and now simply because there was a child involved. There'd always been children in his life. Children who weren't his. If Quinn was willing to be brave about it, then so was he. A relationship didn't have to mean a family and he was sure he could keep the two separate. Especially when the arrangements were all so fluid.

When they'd eaten their fill they headed to the indoor exhibits they'd bypassed in favour of some of the more exotic creatures.

'We are now entering the Rainforest Life,' he said in the style of a nature documentary voiceover artist.

Simon ran ahead into the tropical wilderness, hopped up on mini-desserts and fruit juice.

'He's going to have one hell of a crash when that sugar rush wears off.' Quinn attempted to scold him but he knew she'd savoured every mouthful of that lunch. Each heavenly groan and lick of her lips attested to her pleasure as well as increasing his discomfort. He'd heard those sounds before and intended for her to make them again soon, somewhere more private.

'Look at him!' Simon was off again, following the path of a bright blue bird flitting through the plants and vines.

'He's pretty.' Quinn was observing the exotic display from the balcony beside him, unaware she was adding to the beauty of it all.

Never mind the rare birds flying overhead or the small monkeys swinging freely through the vines, this was all about Quinn for him. The pure delight she took in her surroundings was refreshing and contagious. He'd been so caught up in material possessions and showing he could cut it as a single man in the city, he'd forgotten what it was to just enjoy life. The barrier he'd erected to protect himself had become as much of a prison as that council flat in Dublin.

Given the chance he'd swap his fancy car to travel on a barge anywhere if she was part of the deal. It was as if he was recapturing that lost childhood of his too, by being with her.

He'd been forced to grow up too quickly. From his mother walking out on her family, through his father's illness, and ultimately his death, Matt had never had time for the mischief and fun other kids had experienced. With Quinn he didn't have to be embarrassed in his joy at a puppet show when she was here spinning around, letting the mist fall on her face and telling the sloth how sleepy he looked. Matt had had enough of being the adult and there was plenty of room for his inner child, not to mention the randy teenager.

They stepped out of the light and moved into the nocturnal area. Faced with the creatures of the night, including giant rats and flitting bats, it wasn't long before he found Quinn cuddled up next to him.

'I don't know how Simon is enjoying this.'

'He's a boy. We like gross stuff.'

'I don't want to stay in here,' she whispered, fear pitching her voice until only the bats could probably hear.

Matt felt her hand graze by his knuckles as she fumbled for his reassurance in the dark. He took hold of her and turned so she could make him out in the dimmed light.

'I'll keep you safe.'

In that moment they were locked into their own world, staring into each other's eyes and holding hands like lovers who'd just sworn their lives to one another. The rest of the group had moved on, leaving them alone so the only sounds he could hear now were scurrying animals and the frantic beat of his heart for Quinn.

He cupped her face in his hands and found her mouth easily with his, honing in as if she was a beacon of light guiding him home. This time, instead of pushing him away, she wound her arm around his neck and pulled him closer. He dropped his hands to her waist as she sought him with her tongue and leaned her soft curves against him.

'Have you seen this? He's got really big eyes.' The sound of Simon's voice from across the room somewhere broke through the darkness, alerting them to his presence and throwing a bucket of cold water over them.

'I think that's a bush baby.' Matt's breath was ragged as he fought to regain control so Simon wouldn't think anything was amiss.

'We should probably follow the rest on to the next exhibit.' Quinn was already backing away from him.

'We'll talk about this later,' he whispered, low enough so only she would hear.

'I'm a mum. I have mum things to do.' That uncertainty was back in her wavering voice and Matt fumbled for her hand again in the blackness. He didn't want the guilt to start eating away at her for enjoying a moment of her own.

'Don't forget, the adult fun starts after the *real* dark.' This wasn't over and although she couldn't see him wink, he was sure he sensed her smile.

Somehow they'd find a way to be together without compromising their roles in Simon's life.

His peace of mind depended on it.

Quinn stumbled back out towards Simon and the rest of the visitors tripping out of the exhibit. Her unsteadiness on her feet was more to do with Matt's epic bone-melting prowess than the unfamiliar territory. He had a way of completely knocking her off balance when she was least expecting it.

Yes, she'd encouraged him with a few flirtatious gestures, but phew, that had taken hot to a whole new level. Wrapped in his embrace she'd forgotten who she was, where she was or what day of the week it was, and let the chemistry consume her.

Dangerous. Irresponsible. Intoxicating.

It only made her crave more.

If Simon hadn't reminded them that they weren't here alone, they could've created quite a scene. They were lucky he hadn't seen anything of their passionate embrace or they would've had some explaining to do. Unfortunately, now as she made her way back into the light, the interruption had left her throbbing with unfulfilled need which only Matt could help relieve.

As he'd pointed out, they had things to say, things to do, but they'd have to wait until Simon was safely tucked up in bed and her parental duties were over for the day. The anticipation of where and when they might get to explore this exciting new development uninterrupted was an aphrodisiac in itself. As if she needed it! Quinn was finally starting to believe there could be room in her life for more than foster children. If she dared risk her heart again.

Simon's pace began to slow up and it struck her for the first time about how much energy this day had taken out of him. Not that his enthusiasm had waned once.

'Can we go to the shop now?' His eyes were wide and it was no wonder. A building stuffed to the rafters with soft toys and souvenirs was probably one of the highlights for most of the children. For her, there'd been many others. With one in particular still lingering on her lips, and she wasn't talking about the cakes.

'Sure. What do you say about taking in the rest of the way from a giraffe's point of view?' Matt, obviously picking up on his sudden weariness too, stooped down and gently hoisted Simon up onto his shoulders. It was a balancing act to avoid jarring Simon's right side but he managed it, holding on to make sure his passenger was comfortable and secure.

Rather than make a fuss, he'd found a way to turn a potential meltdown into something fun. A tired and cranky tot was just as difficult to reason with as a frightened, injured one.

Crisis averted, Simon perched happily on Matt's broad shoulders for the remainder of their walk around the grounds with a hand resting on his head. If either of them were in any discomfort they made no mention of it. The smiling twosome blended into the crowd of other fathers and sons and Quinn had to remind herself it was an illusion. It wasn't real. Matt wasn't always going to be around, but for now, it was good for Simon to have someone other than her who actually wanted the best for him.

'I wanna get down.' He only became restless once they reached the shop entrance, so Quinn helped Matt lift him off his shoulders so they could let him loose.

Matt cricked his neck from side to side and massaged his neck. 'I'm getting too old for that.'

'Never.' She got the impression he'd done this sort of thing a lot for his kid sisters. It seemed a shame he was so set on making sure he never committed to fatherhood again. He'd have made a great dad for some lucky child.

'My thirty-five-year-old aching muscles beg to differ. You, on the other hand, strike me as someone who's young at heart and never too old to appreciate these.' He lifted a cuddly bush baby, its big eyes begging Quinn to take him home.

'It's so cute.' She hugged it close, unable to resist the aww factor.

'And a souvenir from our time in the night life exhibit.' His devilish arched eyebrow and wicked smirk immediately flicked her swoon switch.

She'd never been a bad girl, always on her best behaviour, trying to please people so they wouldn't have cause to reject her. Matt drew out that reckless side she'd suppressed for so long and she kind of liked it.

She knew the score. Unlike Darryl, Matt had never said he'd stick around and raise foster kids with her. He was going to leave no matter what.

She didn't have to be a good girl where he was concerned, and based on previous experience he had a hell of a naughty side she wouldn't mind getting to know better. Arousal rushed through her like a warm summer breeze, bringing promises of hot sweaty nights to follow.

It would've been futile to try and stop him from taking the poignant reminder of their day together over to the cash register when he hadn't let her pay for anything so far. She went to look for Simon, who'd disappeared behind the shelving at the front of the shop, probably lining up a selection of animal friends he'd talk Matt into buying for him.

When she walked around the corner she was horrified to find him in tears, surrounded by a group of older boys.

'What's going on?' She went straight into mama bear mode, defending her young and putting a barrier between Simon and whatever was upsetting him.

The three backed off, still laughing, and tossed

a plastic monkey face mask at her feet. 'The freak might look better with one of those.'

At that point Matt came striding over, a formidable figure with a thunderous look on his face which sent Simon's tormentors scurrying out of the shop. 'Are you two okay?'

Quinn was winded from the cruelty she'd witnessed directed at Simon but she hugged him close, letting his tears soak through her dress.

'He's only a baby,' she gasped to Matt, her own tears bubbling to the surface.

They'd had a lovely day and now the actions of some stupid kids had set them back at square one, undoing all the progress they'd made by bringing him here.

Matt crouched down so he was level with Simon's bowed head. 'Hey, wee man. Don't you listen to them.'

Every jerky sob broke her heart a little bit more as Simon clung to her with his one good arm. If she had her way she'd wrap him up in cotton wool so this kind of thing would never happen again. A child this young shouldn't have had to go through so much in his short life.

'No one's ever going to want to be my mummy and daddy because of my stupid face.'

The emotional punch of Simon's words knocked them both into silence.

That belief was at the very heart of the child's fears and why he wouldn't let anyone get too close. He genuinely thought his injuries made him unlovable and that few minutes of taunting had given credence to his worries.

This time Quinn was forced to swipe away a rogue tear but she steeled herself against any more. For her to become an emotional wreck now wasn't going to do Simon any favours.

'Well, I know people who think the world of you. Why else would they have bought you your very own spider monkey?' Matt opened the long arms of the cuddly primate and attached them around Simon's neck. 'I've got some zoo mugs for us too. Why don't we go back to my house to test them out?'

Simon glanced up at her with puffy, red, irresistible eyes. 'Can we?'

'Sure,' she said as brightly as she could muster, thankful that the master of distraction had found a quick and simple way to ease his immediate pain. It was going to have to be down to her to find the long-term solution and show him how loved he was.

Matt stood up and spoke quietly for her ears only. 'I know this wasn't in the plan but my place is closer. We can get a taxi there, get him calmed down again before we get you home.'

She nodded, afraid to verbalise her thanks in case she burst into grateful tears.

Just as he'd reassured Simon, he took her hand and squeezed it. 'Everything's going to be grand.'

She didn't know why but even in the most trying circumstances she believed him.

'Take us home, Matt.' She sighed, content to let the pretence go on a while longer.

CHAPTER EIGHT

THE BACK OF a taxi was a luxury compared to the packed trains or buses at rush hour. The busy streets somehow seemed further away from the sanctity of their private black carriage. It was a shame Quinn's mind couldn't defend against the outside stresses as well as the thick glass windows.

The tears had dried on Simon's face now as he played with the stuffed animals on his lap. Finally sharing what had been troubling him seemed to have taken a weight off his mind, but it hadn't eased hers any. She'd been digging for so long to find out the cause of his inner turmoil she'd imagined it would bring relief. That they would deal with it and move on, naively thinking it would make her better equipped to help him. Far from it. She knew all too well that fear of never belonging, never being loved, and how it never really left, not completely. Despite the efforts of those who'd eventually taken her in. She was always waiting for that moment of final rejection which repeated itself over and over. It had to be the same for Simon, even before his injuries were added to fears which weren't completely unfounded.

Adoption was a long and complicated process and the odds of finding a family for him could well have been worsened with his serious medical, and probable future psychological, problems which not everyone would be willing to take on. Her heart ached for him, and between her and Matt, they had to work together to help him transition into the next phase of the process and find his for ever family.

Matt's home was everything she'd expected it to be on arrival—modern, expensive and in the busy hub of the city—everything hers wasn't. His apartment spoke volumes about their contrasting lifestyles and future plans. He was very much enjoying his freedom as a man about town, whilst her Victorian terraced house had been built with family predominantly in mind.

The floor-to-ceiling windows were impressive, as was the view of the river, but for her it lacked the personal touch, the evidence of family, to make it a home.

However, Matt did his best to make them comfortable for the short time they'd be here. She was certain he'd never intended for them to cross his threshold and this had been nothing more than an emergency stop to prevent her going home with the company of a distressed child to look forward to. Yet, here he was washing up after home-made omelettes and freshly squeezed orange juice as though he'd expected them for dinner all along.

'Were you a Boy Scout? You're always prepared, no matter what catastrophe I bring to your door.' Literally, in this case.

Matt laughed as he stacked the dishwasher. 'I'm no Boy Scout. I still do a big weekly shop, a left-over habit from having a houseful of ravenous teenagers, I suppose.'

'Well, I appreciate it and apparently Simon

does too.' She passed him an empty plate. At least Simon's appetite was improving despite the new drama.

'It's not a problem. Actually, it's been a while since I cooked for anyone. I forgot how much I enjoy doing it.' He leaned against the kitchen worktops and for the first time looked almost unhappy about living on his own.

'Are you seriously telling me you haven't brought women back to show all of this off? Most men would have photos of this as their profile picture all over social media.' Not that he would need to use his money to draw interest. A man who could cook and clean, on top of everything else, was designed for seducing women, her included. No matter how much he tried to hide it, domesticity was very much a part of him.

'I didn't say that. I've just never cooked for any of them. That's what expensive restaurants are for.' The wink he gave her made her sick to the stomach thinking of the women who'd been here before her under entirely different circumstances.

'I guess I'm more one for home-cooked meals

than whatever's fashionable.' She sniffed, despising those who'd put more store in the material things Matt could give them instead of appreciating the qualities which made him who he was—a kind-hearted, generous man, with the patience of a saint. A man she was falling much too hard for and yet she was powerless to stop herself. She was unable to resist when there was still so much to discover about him, and herself.

He'd been generous with his time where Simon was concerned but his support had also boosted her confidence that she wasn't the only stand-in parent in history who'd struggled. As everything in her life had been, this was a rough patch she simply had to fight her way through and that was something she was well practiced in.

'Hey, I only break out the chef's apron for very special guests.' Matt held her chin between his thumb and forefinger and parted her lips.

Her eyelids were already fluttering shut before he settled his mouth on hers, much too briefly. She peered over his shoulder to see how much of this little moment Simon had witnessed. It wouldn't do to have two of them confused about what was happening between her and Matt.

'I think the excitement's all got too much for him.' Matt followed her gaze to the small figure hunched up on the end of the leather sofa.

'How on earth am I going to get him home now?' Although it was a blessed relief to see him so soundly asleep, she didn't relish the thought of having to wake him to get him home and run the risk of him not getting back to sleep again.

'You know what they say, let sleeping five-year-olds lie.' Matt didn't appear to be in a hurry for her to leave, unmoving from his position in the open-plan living room between her and her sleeping babe.

'I think you'll find that's dogs,' she said, gently nudging him aside so she could go and check on Simon.

'It won't do him any harm to sleep there for a while. I swear I'll take you both home as soon as he's awake.' He crossed his heart. 'Scout's promise.'

She narrowed her eyes at him but he did make

her laugh. 'He can't be comfortable in that position though.'

He was curled into the foetal position, his head bent awkwardly over the arm of the chair. It was cramp waiting to happen. Worse, it could aggravate his injuries if he lay like that too long.

'I can move him into the spare bedroom. There's plenty of space for him to stretch out there and sleep undisturbed.'

'You'll have to be careful not to wake him.' She hovered as Matt scooped him up into his big strong arms as though he weighed nothing.

'Don't worry, he's sound asleep.'

Simon didn't so much as flinch as they transferred him down the hall, his arms and legs hanging limply from Matt's hold. The fresh air had obviously done him the world of good.

Matt elbowed the door open and Quinn couldn't have been more surprised about what lay behind it if she'd found an S&M dungeon rigged up. The room was decorated in pretty pinks and purples, flowers and fairies, and everything he'd said he'd despised in home décor growing up. At the far side of the room next to a mountain of children's toys and teddy bears was a child-sized bed and a white wooden cot. The perfect little girl's room and nursery.

'Is there something you want to tell me?' He'd made such a big production about not wanting family responsibilities, she hoped she wasn't about to discover he was, in fact, a divorced dad of two little girls. She didn't think she could handle it if he'd lied to her about who he was when that was the very man she'd fallen for.

He carefully laid Simon on top of the bed covers and pulled a comforter over him before he attempted to explain himself.

'I told you I have sisters. Anne, the eldest, is married with two daughters, Jaime and Lucy. Sometimes they come visit.' He fussed around, closing the curtains and making sure the floor was clear of any debris Simon could trip over.

It was a far cry from the self-centred bachelor he'd portrayed and she wondered why he'd withheld this snippet of information. Perhaps his family situation would have put off a different type of woman, one who'd have been horrified at the thought of being required to babysit or change dirty nappies someday. Not her.

She backed out of the room with a snigger. 'So, basically, you're a granddad?'

Matt rolled his eyes and closed the door softly behind him. 'See? This is why I don't generally share the details of my personal life. It changes the way people see me. I have two sides. To the outside world I'm a young, single, successful surgeon. To my family, I'm an agony aunt and a doting uncle. I don't tend to let the two worlds collide.'

'And which side am I seeing?' They were standing toe to toe in the hallway and Quinn was sure he could hear her heart thumping against her ribcage. The more she got to know the *real* Matt, the more she wanted to believe they stood a chance of making this work.

'Well, Quinn, you are an anomaly.' He reached out and tucked a strand of her hair behind her ear. 'Somehow you've managed to set a foot in both camps and I'm not sure how I feel about that.'

It was the kind of honesty she appreciated. He wasn't promising her the world to get what he wanted, only telling her that she'd made him think about what they were getting into and that was enough for now.

'Me either.' She didn't know what each step further into his life meant for her down the line except more heartache but for now the one thing she was sure of was that she wanted him.

She leaned closer but Matt was already there to meet her, meshing his lips with hers as though they'd always meant to fit together.

Her conscience drifted between taking him by the hand and leading him to the bedroom, or setting up camp outside Simon's door in case he needed her. 'What about Simon? What if he wakes up and doesn't know where he is?'

She couldn't blame Matt for wanting to avoid ready-made families when they were such a passion killer at the most inopportune moments. Every time their make-out sessions got steamy it seemed to trigger the baby alarm.

No hanky-panky! You have a child to think about!

Not what any hot-blooded man wanted interrupting his love life and Matt wouldn't have any trouble finding a willing partner elsewhere if he kept getting sex-blocked by a five-year-old and his panicky mum.

She was already preparing herself for the 'This isn't going to work' speech as Matt took off towards the living room. She trudged behind him and wondered how they were going to put the time in during Simon's unexpected nap now. A game of chess perhaps? Or maybe he had a photo album of all of his glamorous, readily available exes she could flick through while they waited. If she'd had a coat she would've fetched it.

'I have one of these.' Instead of his sex life in pictures, he produced a baby monitor and set it on the coffee table with a proud flourish as if he'd solved the world's hardest equation. For her, he had.

No matter what obstacles crept up he always found a way over them. He didn't quit at the first sign of trouble and that was new to her as far as men were concerned. It was difficult not to get too attached to someone who, so far, had done everything possible to show her she could trust him. Rely on him.

'Of course you do,' she said with a great big grin.

All the signs were pointing to a brother and uncle who took his family duties very seriously even if he didn't want people to know. He was a loving family man whether he liked it or not. It was the idea of taking on someone else's which was the sticking point for him, and prevented any notion of a relationship between them.

'I'll just nip in and turn on the one in the bedroom so we can hear if he gets up. I'll be two seconds.'

Quinn took a seat on the sofa to wait for him coming back, fidgeting with the hem of her dress and unable to sit still, thinking about what was going to happen next as if she was waiting for her first kiss.

Things with Matt had gone far beyond that.

This would be the only quality time they'd spent together alone and she was afraid it mightn't live up to the hype of that fevered embrace in the dark corner of the zoo.

He wanted her to stick around. He'd told her there was more to come. Surely the next step they were about to take wasn't all in her head?

'Would you like a drink?' Matt was back, padding into the kitchen.

'A glass of water would be nice, thanks.' Suddenly, her tongue was sticking to the roof of her mouth and her hands were clammy. Just what every guy was looking for in a hot date. Not.

She thought of all those other women he'd had here who'd never seen the kitchen. They were probably too busy ripping his clothes off in a frenzy to get to the bedroom to care. She must seem so dull in comparison but she no longer saw herself as sexy, spending her days watching cartoons and washing dirty clothes, lucky if she'd had a chance to brush her hair that morning, so why should she expect a man to?

At least with advance warning she'd be spending the day with Matt, she'd been able to put an effort into her clothes and make-up today. It couldn't hurt to try and reconnect with her inner sex siren, who'd disappeared under a mountain of paperwork and rejection.

The sofa dipped as Matt sat down next to her and handed her a glass of water. She took a sip and flicked her tongue out to wet her parched lips, fully aware he was watching her every move. He reached up to rub the back of his neck and Quinn seized the opportunity to get physical.

'Turn around and I'll give you a quick massage. You've earned one after all the carrying you've done today.' She set her glass on the floor and kicked off her shoes so she could kneel on the couch beside him.

'I probably should have stretched before I started bench pressing dead weights.' He turned around so she was faced with the solid wall of his back. She bit back the comment about bench pressing her anytime in case that bordered more on the side of desperate and crass rather than sexy and irresistible. This too-long abstinence had really brought out the worst in her.

With trembling hands she kneaded his shoulders, the thick muscle resisting her attempts to manipulate the tissue.

'Perhaps you should...er...take your shirt off. You're really knotted up in there.' Not very subtle and as bold as she dared but he complied nonetheless, shrugging the shirt off over his head.

'Wow,' she mouthed as she got to see the impressive physique beneath for the first time in the flesh, albeit from the back. If only she could find the excuse to start massaging the pecs she knew would be on the other side of that muscular frame.

She worked her fingers over his warm skin, smoothing her hand down the length of his spine until she reached the waistband of his jeans. With a sudden burst of bravado, or lust, she slid her hand beneath and reached around until she felt that smooth V of taut skin leading down to...

Matt sucked in a sharp breath and clapped his

hand over hers, stopping her pathetic seduction attempt dead in its tracks.

'I'm sorry...I...' What? How the hell was she going to pass this off as anything other than a blatant grope?

She rocked back on her heels, contemplating a commando-style roll onto the floor so she could crawl away without having to look him in the eye again, but he had too firm a grip on her wrist.

He spun around so she had no option but to face him. Okay, it wasn't all bad; she'd got a sneak peek at the goods, but she would need something good to remember anytime she replayed this humiliation in her head. For the record, she was pretty sure they'd used a mould of his chest and abs for those superhero costumes with the fake muscles.

'You don't have to try so hard, Quinn.' He was smiling, not recoiling in disgust, which she took as a good omen.

'Wh-what do you mean?' She tossed her hair back, aiming for the nonchalance of a woman who stuck her hand down a man's pants whenever she felt like it.

'You don't have to force this. Let it happen naturally.' In slow motion he moved closer until his breath whispered on her lips, turning her to a rag doll liable to slip off the furniture in a cascade of molten limbs. She closed her eyes and let nature take its course.

He captured her in a soft kiss, leaned her back against the cushions as he took possession of her. It was true—there was no need for planning or acting out a part she thought she needed to play when chemistry did all the work.

Quinn was lying flat out beneath him, clinging to him, although there was no chance of going anywhere with his weight pinning her down. They were both where they needed to be.

She'd surprised him by taking the lead when, to date, she'd been the one reluctant to let this go further than snatched kisses. It wasn't unwelcome, parts of him were throbbing with delight, but he'd needed to take back some control. Not of her, or the situation, but of himself.

He was getting too caught up in her and Simon. Although bringing them back here had been more of an intervention than an invitation into his personal life, the result had been the same. They were invading his personal space, and his heart.

He'd raged inside today after Simon had been bullied by those kids, ached for him, and Quinn, who'd had to deal with the fallout. All he'd wanted to do was take some of that pain away, regardless that it meant compromising himself in the process.

If he took his own advice and simply let this thing take its natural course he could find himself saddled with more parental duties he hadn't asked for. That's why he needed a clear head, to focus on something other than his own pleasure—Quinn's.

These big blue eyes peered up at him with such trust and longing it was a test of strength not to take the easy route to instant gratification and sod the consequences. Even though it was killing him, this self-punishment would serve as a reminder to him not to start something he couldn't finish. Like getting involved with a single mother.

Quinn didn't have any such reservations as she pulled him ever closer until his chest was crushing hers, her soft mounds rubbing against him and undoing his restraint bit by bit. Eager to feast his eyes on her naked flesh, he slipped the shoestring straps of her dress down her arms and peeled away her strapless bra. Her cherry-peaked breast fit easily into the palm of his hand, so ripe and ready he couldn't resist a taste. He took her in his mouth and suckled her sweetness.

He shifted his position slightly so the evidence of his arousal wasn't so uncomfortable for either of them but Quinn tilted her hips so it nestled between her thighs instead. He released her sensitive nub with a groan as his resolve eroded by the second, clearly underestimating the effect she'd have on him even with his trousers firmly buttoned up. A fact which hadn't gone unnoticed by a partner who was doing her best to address that problem, popping his buttons open one by one.

This woman was driving him crazy and if he

wasn't careful his good intentions would soon give way to lust, a short-term solution to his current predicament but undoubtedly with long-term consequences. He needed to bring this to some sort of conclusion which made her feel good without giving too much of himself in the process.

He inched his hand up her thigh and, with a quick tug, divested her of her undies. Her giggle as he tossed them onto the floor only spurred him on in his devilment. With a trail of kisses, over her clothes this time, he made his way down the centre of her body and ducked his head under the skirt of her dress.

'Matt—' she gasped, her hands immediately lighting atop his head, but she didn't ask him to stop.

He took his time savouring that first taste of her, teasing his tongue along her folds before parting her to thrust inside her core. She bucked against him, drawing him deeper between her thighs. He cupped her buttocks, holding her in place so he could direct his attention straight to that sweet spot.

He circled that little nub of flesh, sucking and licking his way to heaven until her breathy pants almost brought him to climax too. She tightened around him and he could sense that impending release. Her fingers were digging into his shoulders, her body rising and falling with the clench and release of her inner muscles.

She was slick with arousal, inviting him to join with her on the climb to that final peak but he couldn't take the chance he'd never want to come back down to earth. He withdrew, only to plunge back inside her again, and again, until she came apart beneath him. It was a shame he couldn't hear her cries of ecstasy as she slapped a hand over her mouth to muffle the sound. There was nothing he wanted more than to hear and see her completely undone, not holding anything back and without a trace of self-consciousness, but he understood why she couldn't turn off that mothering instinct. When he was long gone, she still had Simon to think about.

He sat back, giving Quinn space to recover as she fought to catch her breath, and a chance to regain his own composure. Not an easy task when her face was flushed, her pupils dilated and she was still half naked.

The lights on the baby monitor flashed, accompanied by the sound of rustling sheets, saving Matt from himself. Simon was stirring and he'd made a vow to get them home the minute that happened. It was his get-out clause before he did something even more stupid than falling for this beautiful woman he'd just ravished on his sofa.

'I'll go check on him,' he told her, keen to get a minute alone to gather his thoughts now both of their worlds had been rocked.

'Thanks.' Quinn sat up and adjusted her clothes to cover her nakedness, suddenly bashful. She'd no need to be embarrassed. He was the one who'd screwed up.

Whether he'd given in to temptation or not he'd still fallen for the one woman he couldn't have. Quinn came as part of a package deal, and although he was fond of Simon, there was every chance her foster brood could expand later on and he wasn't signing up for that. He hadn't left his family to move out to London only to have his longed-for independence curtailed by someone else's children.

He and Quinn were on completely different paths but they couldn't seem to stop intersecting and complicating things. Something had to give and it sure as hell wasn't going to be his freedom. Whilst he was treating Simon, cutting off all contact was out of the question, even if he thought he could.

The whole day had been an eye-opener for him but his resistance had been stretched to breaking point for now. If he didn't get his house guests back to their own home soon, he'd find this slipping into a long-term arrangement and this was supposed to be his time, a new start. He wasn't going to fall into the same old trap.

Matt McGrory was young, free and single, and that was the way it would stay. He just had to keep chanting that mantra to himself so he'd start believing it, or find someone else to take his place in Quinn and Simon's affections.

CHAPTER NINE

THE LAST FEW days had passed Quinn by in an out-of-body, did-that-actually-happen? daze.

There had to be a catch somewhere in a man who'd spent the day piggybacking a five-year-old around the zoo, and at night had made her pleasure his sole purpose. At this moment in time she didn't care what that flaw might be when her body was still glowing from the after-effects of his attentions.

Even now, another delicious shudder rippled through her at the memory of his lips on her. The only problem was, she hadn't seen the man of the moment since. She'd convinced herself it was because he was so busy at work, too invested to believe what they'd shared could be ignored so easily.

She turned her face away from the patients and

staff walking towards her in the hospital corridor in case they read her X-rated thoughts. Her infatuation with the surgeon was probably there on her smiling face for the world to see and she could do without lectures from do-gooders who might take it upon themselves to warn her off a man committed to bachelorhood. They couldn't tell her anything she hadn't already told herself.

You're going to get hurt. He won't commit.

She didn't want to hear it when it was all too late anyway. She was in love with Matt and for once she didn't want to think about the consequences. That day had shown her how important it was for her to take some time for herself and that didn't always have to include getting naked with Matt, as enjoyable as that had been. The smallest thing such as a chat, a meal or a walk without stressing about Simon's issues had made her feel lighter than she had in months. A state of mind which would benefit them both.

Simon had been much more content the next morning than usual. The day's exertions had meant he'd slept through the night, even after

Matt had driven them home, and the rarity of his uninterrupted sleep had improved the atmosphere between them.

To date, she hadn't availed of any outside help to care for her boy. She'd wanted to prove she could manage on her own and turned down any offers of respite care in case it disrupted Simon any further. There was also the fear that it would highlight her inadequacies even more. Now she was beginning to rethink those ideas of extra support.

That was how she'd come to be at the hospital now without her little bundle of curls in tow. He'd been excited when she'd suggested he could spend some time with Mrs Johns, as had her widowed neighbour when she'd broached the subject of babysitting. She was on the list of approved contacts with the authorities as she'd volunteered to help from day one when she found out there'd be a little one in the street. Quinn had only given her name in case she needed someone at a moment's notice in an emergency but perhaps she and Simon needed to venture beyond the bubble they'd created for themselves since the fire.

No doubt he'd be spoiled and filled to the brim with home-baked goods by the time she returned, but a young boy should have doting elders, play-dates and adventures. A grown woman should have coffee mornings, gossip and a love life where possible. It was time to bring some normality back into their lives.

Of course, she'd seen to her other responsibilities before she'd gone in search of the man who'd convinced her she didn't need to remain celibate in order to be a good mother.

She'd added her voice to the ongoing protest out front for the first shift of the day and she'd had a ball this time with the knowledge that Simon was safe and happy. There was a rush of feel-good endorphins from volunteering her services to a good cause and they didn't come any greater than trying to save this iconic building from decimation. Perhaps she could make this a regular thing and when Simon went back to school permanently she might think about volunteering somewhere else that might need her help. They were already in the process of rebuilding the school and she would need something to distract her when it was time for him to go back there.

For now, she was collecting personal statements from some of the parents she'd seen coming and going on a regular basis.

'That's fantastic. I really appreciate your help,' she said, adding another paper bullet to the committee's arsenal of weapons against the board's decision.

'Anything I can do to help. We'd be lost without this place and we've made so many friends here I can't imagine starting over somewhere new.' Mrs Craig's daughter, Penny, was a regular feature around the Castle's corridors, an outpatient but still dependent on oxygen at all times. Quinn had heard on the grapevine she was waiting for a life-saving heart transplant.

'Neither can I.' She'd spent those first days after the fire praying Simon would pull through, not eating or sleeping until she knew for sure he was going to survive. What Mrs Craig and

Penny had been through, still had to go through, didn't bear thinking about. For her treatment to be transferred elsewhere away from the staff, who'd probably become like family, would be a wrench. Quinn knew how it was to rely on these people, get closer than she should, and how devastating it would be when they were no longer part of her life.

This was exactly the kind of emotional impact the money men didn't stop to consider when they were cost-cutting and paper shuffling.

'Are you Simon's mum?' The little girl in question wheeled her way in between the two adults, demanding attention, though she was difficult to ignore dressed in her pink tutu anyway.

'Yes. I'm his foster mum, Quinn. Pleased to meet you.' She held out her hand to shake on their introduction.

'I'm Penny and I know everyone here,' she said matter-of-factly.

'And quite the celebrity, I believe.' Quinn gave the mother a knowing smile. All of the kids had their own way of coping with life on the wards but Penny's integration into the hospital community and her self-confidence was something she envied on Simon's behalf.

'Nosy, more like,' Mrs Craig muttered under her breath.

'You're seeing Matt, aren't you?' Penny tilted her head to one side to study her.

Quinn's cheeks were on fire. She hadn't been able to keep her feelings hidden for long. Goodness knew how he'd react when he saw her again if it was plain enough for a child to see she was mad about him. He probably wouldn't be renewing any local contracts again soon, that was for sure.

'Er—'

'He's not here today. I wanted to show him my new tiara but Rebecca says he's off today.' She patted the pretty plastic band perched on her head as if it was a perfectly good reason for Matt to make time to see her—though knowing him, he probably would.

'Penny, I'm sure you're supposed to be doing

something other than gossiping in the corridor. Come on and let Quinn get on with her job.'

'Okay, okay.' She spun her chair around towards the elevator.

Quinn gave her thanks again and waved goodbye. The news about Matt's sudden absence had unsettled her all over again.

He hadn't said anything that night about taking time off. In hindsight, he hadn't said much after Simon had woken up. She'd been too caught up in her own orgasmic euphoria and subsequent worry about getting Simon home without disturbing him too much to contemplate Matt's state of mind. He'd given so much without taking anything for himself. Whilst she'd taken so much pleasure in his unselfishness in the moment, now she was scrutinising his motives. Very few men would've been happy to be left unattended to and it wasn't because he'd been immune to the heat of the moment. She'd seen and felt the hard evidence of his arousal against her.

They could've found a way to be together. If Matt had suggested she and Simon stayed the night she would've jumped at the chance. His readiness to get rid of all traces of them from his apartment didn't marry with her idea of carrying on where they'd left off.

Okay, he was never going to declare his undying love and set up house with them but it didn't bode well if he needed time off to recover after only a few hours in their company.

It wasn't as if he lived a million miles away. Her brain flashed through all the possibilities his actions could mean. She wanted to make it clear she wasn't expecting anything from him other than what they already had together.

All she wanted was a little more time together to explore what was happening between them and the effect it was having on her. Emotional significance aside, if they focused on the physical progression of their relationship they could have a good time together before his contract ended and he disappeared for good. If nothing else, she needed to return the favour he'd done her. She didn't like to be in anyone's debt.

She started off at a brisk pace towards the

shiny, modern apartment block with her sights set on ripping Matt's clothes off and seducing him. Unfortunately, the doubt crows soon caught up with her, flapping their wings in her face to slow her down.

Did she really have the right to turn up, unannounced, on his doorstep? He could be sick, or perhaps this wasn't about her at all. There were a multitude of reasons he might not want to see her right now.

She could stand outside staring through the glass of the lobby like a child at a toy shop window on Christmas Eve, or she could stop wasting her precious time and find out the answer.

With her finger poised to buzz him, she braced herself to start overanalysing the tone of his voice over the intercom. The door suddenly swung open and one of the residents held it open for her. Clearly she wasn't a threat to anyone's security—except, perhaps, her own.

'Thanks,' she said as Mr Suit rushed on to whatever meeting he was going to, paying no mind to who he'd let into his building.

Every crisp step along the marble hallway towards Matt's apartment made her stomach roll more violently. If anyone from the hospital was aware she was here they'd probably advise him to get a restraining order. He was Simon's surgeon. Then again, what they'd shared that night broke whatever rules and boundaries long before she'd walked in off the street.

She took a deep breath before she knocked on the door, not knowing what to expect from this encounter. He mightn't even be home. After all, he had family and doctor commitments she wasn't party to. It wasn't likely he'd take time off at short notice to sit at home in the shadows to avoid running into a one-night stand, or whatever she was to him. If he wasn't in she could pretend this had never happened and let him make the next move.

Suddenly, the door whooshed open and her breath was sucked into a vacuum.

'Quinn! The very person I need to speak to.'

Not the welcome she'd expected, particularly

as he was slamming his front door shut behind him and jangling his car keys.

'I...er...you haven't been around much—'

'I know. I know. Wait, where's Simon?'

'He's staying with a neighbour. I thought we could both do with a playdate this morning.' With one obviously going better than the other.

'Good idea,' he said, but he was still walking away from his apartment rather than dragging her back inside.

'I can see you're busy. Maybe we'll catch up another time.' She could salvage some dignity if she walked away now without forcing a conversation about what significance she held in his life. She had her answer right here with a closed door in her face.

Matt slowed his brisk pace as if it had only occurred to him how odd her visit was. 'You didn't make the journey all the way here just to see me, did you?'

It sounded such a desperate act when he put it that way that she immediately had to deny it. 'No. I was at the hospital anyway helping the committee. Young Penny said she'd heard you'd taken some leave. I thought I'd call in and see if you were sick or something.' If she'd stopped to buy grapes on the way here she might've made that more plausible.

He laughed. 'Ah, yes. Penny. There are no secrets where she's concerned.'

'I was collecting statements from the parents.' That was right up there with 'I carried a watermelon' in lame excuses but she didn't want him to think she'd been stalking the corridors seeking him out.

'They're definitely one of the most familiar families at Paddington's and Penny is such a live wire despite her condition.' He was clearly fond of the little girl even though she wasn't one of his own patients. Another indication that his devotion went far beyond the parameters of his job description.

'She is and I can report back and tell her you're fine and there's no need for her to worry.' Quinn scooted outside into the sunlight first, taking the path back to the hospital so she didn't trip on her lies. It was her who'd wanted to know why he wasn't at work and her who'd stumble back home with her tail tucked between her legs for thinking she could simply turn up here and take what she wanted from Matt, ignoring his wishes, which clearly included being left alone.

That heavy weight was back on her shoulders, almost doubling her over with the effort of having to carry it again.

'Aren't you coming with me?'

It took a strong hand wrapped around her waist for the words to register.

'Do you want me to? I mean, you were on your way out before I got here.' *Without me.*

'It will make this easier. I would've had to contact you anyway to make the final decision.' He practically bounced into the front seat of his car, pumped up by whatever he had planned.

'That sounds ominous. Where are we going?'

'It's a surprise. Relax. It's nothing bad. Just sit back and enjoy the ride.'

The car purred to life at his touch, much the way she had.

They stopped and started their way out of the city until eventually they made their way onto the quieter roads. She had no clue how long they were going to be in the car or how far they'd be driving but she didn't care. For now, she was content to sit back and relax in his company as he'd suggested. It wasn't what she'd planned but it was preferable to the scenario where he told her he didn't want to see her again.

She trusted him to give her a good time. He hadn't let her down yet.

Matt was in the dark about what had brought Quinn to his door but her visit was providential. He'd been contemplating a major commitment for her and Simon so it was only polite he should seek her opinion on the matter.

Since that day he'd spent with them, and most of the evening, he'd been trying to concoct a plan to keep them in his life without stepping into the role of surrogate dad again. It would be easy to get carried away, especially when a different part of his body other than his brain was trying to make decisions for him.

If he'd given in to what it was he'd really wanted he'd be in an ever bigger mess where Quinn was concerned. That first-hand experience of bringing up a family was the only thing which had prevented him from taking her to his bed, letting Simon sleep the night in his spare room and waking up to a new domesticity he hadn't asked for. His fear of that had somehow won out over his libido. He couldn't promise that would always be the case so he'd hit on the idea of a third wheel in their relationship, or a fourth if he included Simon.

'A dog pound?' Quinn's raised eyebrows drew into a frown as they pulled up outside the animal rescue centre in a blend of undisguised curiosity and disappointment. Exactly what he'd been trying to avoid.

He'd delayed getting back in touch when he knew nothing he said or did could possibly match up to any expectations she might have had after that night. Now, he was counting on the tried and tested distraction technique of canine cuteness.

'It's an idea I've been toying with. Pet companions are known to be very therapeutic, loving unconditionally without judging people's appearances or background. You saw what a great time Simon had at the zoo. He loves animals and this could really help build his confidence.' It would also give them the sort of close companionship that they were both craving on a long-term basis.

Quinn was silent as they entered the reception and he hoped it was because she was mulling over the idea of adopting a dog, not that she was filled with quiet rage at him.

'It's a nice idea, in theory, but it's not very practical. I have enough to deal with without adding house-training a puppy to the list.'

'This one's a year old, fully trained. No extra work.' A puppy would've secured the deal because who wouldn't fall in love with a bundle of fur but she wouldn't have thanked him for the puddles around the house or using her furniture for oversized chew sticks. He'd been there when Siobhan, his middle sister, had suckered him into housing one of a litter of unwanted pups. Thankfully, she'd taken the little poop machine with her when she'd moved out soon after.

'This one?' She raised an eyebrow, seemingly unimpressed as he showed her the computer printout of his research subject.

'Frankie. She's a collie cross. I saw her online and made this appointment to come and see her before I spoke to you. You know, to make sure she's suitable for you and Simon.' He gave his details to the receptionist and waited for them to bring out the dog he thought could be the answer to everyone's prayers.

'How very thoughtful of you.' The sarcasm wasn't lost on him. It had been very presumptuous of him to make these arrangements, supposedly on her behalf, without giving her the heads-up. He preferred to think of it as being proactive.

'She's supposed to be a lovely wee thing.' He'd made sure this was a dog they could be satisfied was comfortable around children, and from everyone he'd spoken to, she was very good-natured.

'Wee?' Quinn was nearly knocked off her feet by the black-and-tan slobber monster which accosted her.

'Well, those handbag dogs aren't for boys. She's a good sturdy size for cuddling.'

It was his turn to pet the reason they were here and he was rewarded with a rough doggie tongue licking his face.

'What's wrong with her neck?' Quinn hunkered down to inspect the patch of shaved fur and jagged scars zigzagging around her throat.

'They found her wandering the streets. Someone had let the skin grow over her puppy collar and the vet had to operate to remove it. Hence the name "Frankie," after Frankenstein's monster.' He'd seen the pictures and read the case file so she'd already claimed a place in his affections. Quinn's too, by all accounts, as she stroked and cuddled the pooch.

'Poor girl. You deserve a pretty name. If you were mine I'd call you Maisie.'

'Maisie?' He tried to suppress a grin and failed.

The scarred, scrawny mutt looked as girlie as he did.

'Every girl should be treated like a princess. Calling her after a monster will do nothing for her self-esteem. If I'd ever had a daughter, Maisie's the name I would've chosen.' For such a young woman, she sounded as though she'd given up on the idea of ever having kids of her own. Fostering probably seemed enough of a challenge without bringing up her own children minus a partner. Still, if Maisie filled that particular void too, then Matt's job here was done.

'We'll have to bring Simon up for a visit but I can register our interest now in case someone else wants her in the meantime.'

'I'm sure he'll love her, Matt, but would it really be fair to give him a dog only to take it off him when he moves on? I couldn't break his heart again.' She was already distancing herself from the mongrel, who just wanted to be loved too.

Matt hadn't considered the long-term consequences. It was so unlike him to go for the temporary solution, but she was right—he couldn't use the dog as a sticking plaster. The moment Simon had to leave her behind would devastate him all over again and who was to say Quinn would want to be tied down to a pet once Simon had gone.

There was no other option but for him to take her on if he wanted this adoption to go ahead. It was a commitment he'd never anticipated making but a dog had to be less trouble than raising kids, surely?

'What if I adopt her? You and Simon could help with her when I'm at work. He can still bond with her but technically she'll be my dog.' A single man was still a single man with a pet. It would be company for him instead of coming home to that empty apartment at the end of every shift. He'd hate to let this opportunity pass for Simon and Maisie to find some comfort in each other.

'You mean joint custody?' Naturally, Quinn wanted clarification. She was a woman who didn't like to leave room for misunderstandings.

It was surprising, then, that she'd yet to quiz him on his intentions as far as she was concerned.

It was the main reason he'd maintained a little distance because he genuinely didn't know what either of them wanted to come from this relationship. If Quinn in her usual forthright manner told him she expected some sort of commitment to her and Simon, he'd be forced to walk away and he wasn't ready for that yet.

'I guess…' Adopting a stray dog was more than he'd committed to in a long time, stretching the boundaries of his comfort zone and the best promise he could give in regards of a future together.

For the duration of Simon's stay with her, he and Maisie would be a part of their lives and that was the most he could give of himself without compromising his own plans. He'd still be moving on to pastures new someday, except now he'd have a slobbery hound in tow.

'Simon's going to be so excited.' Quinn dropped down to hug the new family friend and Matt didn't know if she or the dog had the biggest smile on their face.

He had to admit he felt good to have been the

one to have orchestrated this. Quinn's happiness was his weakness and most likely guaranteed to be his greatest downfall but he reminded himself he was a live-in-the-moment guy and bundled in on the fun. As he joined the group hug, the excitement proved too much for Maisie, who slipped out of their hold for a mad dash around the room.

'Thank you for this.' Quinn dropped a kiss on his mouth as they tumbled to the ground. He wanted to freeze time, keep her there for ever so they didn't have to worry about anything except keeping that simple contact between them.

When she was with him, touching him, happy to be with him, he wanted to give her the world. He'd already broken all the singleton rules and was about to adopt a stray dog just so this feeling would last. He was afraid of what he would do next in the name of love.

There was no doubt about it. Given the lengths he'd gone to and his wish to lie here with her for ever, he was totally head over heels for Quinn Grady. It should've made him want to bolt from the room, pack his bags and catch the first flight back to Dublin but that wouldn't solve the problem. Wherever he went he knew he'd be thinking of her. The only way to get this out of his system was to let it run its course until they reached some sort of crisis point where having him in her life was no longer tenable. She was going to have to be the one to make that decision because, for once, Matt wasn't the one in charge. His heart was.

CHAPTER TEN

'WE HAVE A small communal garden she can use, and of course there's the nearby park.' Matt's application for Maisie-homing hadn't been as easy as simply signing a form, and rightly so. The animal shelter had insisted on doing a home visit to see for themselves that the ground-floor apartment was a suitable environment for her, and Quinn had agreed to be here for it.

She was still in shock he'd come up with the idea in the first place, never mind taken on primary responsibility of a dog to aid Simon's recovery. An act which certainly wouldn't have been part of his Hippocratic oath. This level of kindness couldn't be taught; it was pure Matt.

She didn't want to get her hopes up, much like she didn't want Simon to get too attached to him, or Maisie. At least by getting Matt to adopt the dog she'd managed to put some sort of safety prevention in place. When their dalliance inevitably came to its unsatisfactory conclusion they could go their separate ways without any ill will or duty to the other. The dog would be his responsibility, and Simon was hers.

'And where will doggie sleep?' The lady with the clipboard peered in the various rooms sussing out what preparations Matt had made for his new house companion.

'This is her bed here and Quinn's going to let her in and out while I'm at work.' Matt proudly showed off the comfy new dog bed full of new toys and treats he and Simon had picked out at the pet store.

It was all Simon could talk about since Matt had told him the news. He'd been clear to point out Maisie would be his but Simon could help out.

'Yes, we'll take her for walks and make sure she gets plenty of exercise when Matt's not here.' It was something she was looking forward to too. It would get them both outdoors more and be a step towards his recovery if the dog had his attention rather than the people around him. All thanks to Matt.

'I'll take a quick look at the garden to make sure it's safe and secure for Maisie but I don't think we'll have any problems giving the adoption the green light.' The lady who held Maisie's future in the palm of her hand gave a thumbs up before she ventured outside.

Quinn breathed a sigh of relief and left Matt to deal with any last-minute details with the inspector. If the process for adopting children was as straightforward it would have made life a lot easier for Simon. He might have found a family and settled down a long time ago if he hadn't been caught up in the bureaucracy for so long. Although that would've meant she'd never have got to meet him, and no matter what hardships they'd endured so far, she couldn't imagine being without him. Evidently she wasn't able to keep her emotions out of any relationship.

For someone who'd only ever meant to provide a safe and loving home for children until they'd found their adoptive families, she'd managed to fall for Simon and Matt along the way. They'd saved her at a time when she'd been at her loneliest. Now she knew how it was to be part of a family, however accidental, however dysfunctional, her life was never going to be the same without either of them. Regardless of what the future held, this was the most content she'd ever been and she'd learned never to take that for granted.

Happiness had come late in her childhood, infrequently in her adulthood, and was something she intended to make the most of for however long she was able to give and receive it.

'I don't think that could've gone any better. It won't be long before we hear that pitter-patter of little feet around here.' Matt was every inch the proud new adoptive dad when he returned.

Quinn would be lying if she said she didn't experience a pang of longing for a man who'd feel that way about children. In an ideal world Matt would be as joyful about the prospect of adding foster children to his family as he was about the dog. Maybe if she had a partner like that to support her she might've found the strength to adopt Simon herself, confident she could give him a more stable life than the one his neglectful parents had provided.

'I should go back. It's not fair on Simon, or Mrs Johns, to make a habit of this.'

'Twice isn't a habit. It's simply making the most of a good thing.' He advanced towards her with a hunger in his eyes that made her pulse quicken as fever took hold of her body.

This was the first time they'd been truly alone with no outside distraction from the simmering sexual attraction and no reason to stop it bubbling over.

'So, it's okay to do something naughty twice without having to worry it's the wrong thing?' She took a step forward to meet him, resting her hands on his chest, desperate to make body contact again.

'Definitely. Especially if you didn't technically *do it* first time around.' He teased her lips with the breath of innuendo, leaving her trembling with anticipation.

'If you say so—' She plucked the top button of his shirt open, ready to get the party started once and for all. They mightn't ever get the chance to do this again and then she really would have regrets. She'd had a sample of how good they could be together and not following it up seemed more idiotic than taking the risk.

If Simon wasn't in the picture she wouldn't hesitate to give herself to Matt and when this was over the only consolation she'd have was that she'd been true to herself.

'I do.' His mouth was suddenly crushing hers, the force of his passion hard and fast enough to make her head spin.

She trembled from the sheer intensity of the embrace as he pulled her close. Her knees went completely from under her as Matt swept her up into his arms, her squeal of surprise quietened by his primitive growl. She clung tightly to him, her hands around his neck, her mouth still meshed to his, afraid to break contact in case she started overthinking this again. When he was touching her it was all that mattered.

He strode down the hallway and she heard the heavy thud as he kicked the bedroom door open to carry her inside. She'd never gone for macho displays but, somehow, knowing the usually un-flappable Matt was so impatient to get her to bed was the greatest turn-on ever.

He booted the door shut behind them again, ensuring they were completely cut off from the rest of the world. There was just her, Matt and a bed built for two.

They fell onto the mattress together, each pull-ing at the other's clothes until they were naked with no barriers left between them. They'd had weeks of foreplay, months if she counted all of those arguments at the hospital, and she didn't want to wait any longer.

She was slick with desire as they rolled across the bed in a tangle of limbs and kisses. Once Matt had sheathed himself in a condom he grabbed from his night stand, he thrust inside her. His hardness found her centre so confidently and securely she knew she'd found her peace.

Matt had finally lost his control, yet joining with Quinn brought him more relief than fear. He'd been strong for too long, trying to do the right thing by everyone when his body had been crying out for this. For Quinn.

He moved slowly inside her at first, testing what little there was left of his restraint, luxuriating in her tight, wet heat. She was a prize he knew he didn't deserve and one he'd only have possession of for a very short time. Quinn was her own woman who wouldn't be so easily swayed by great sex. It would soon become clear he didn't have anything else to bring to the party. If she expected anything more he'd only leave her with extra scars to deal with.

Quinn tightened her grip around his shaft to remind him this wasn't a time for inner reflection and stole the remnants of his control. As much as he wanted to pour inside her he also wanted this to be something she wouldn't regret. This should be a positive experience they could both look back on fondly, not a lapse of judgement they'd come to resent.

They'd gone into this fully aware this wasn't the beginning of some epic love story. No matter how he felt about her this couldn't be about anything more than sex. He could never say he loved her out loud; that would place too much pressure on him to act on it when it wasn't a possibility. He wasn't about to turn his life upside down again for the sake of three little words.

She ground her hips against him, demanding he show her instead. Carnal instinct soon took over from logical thinking as he sought some resolution for them both.

His strokes became quicker with Quinn's mews of pleasure soon matching the new tempo. He captured her moans with a kiss, driving his tongue into her mouth so he had her completely anchored to him. She didn't shy away from his lustful invasion but welcomed it, wrapping her legs around his back to hold him in place.

Matt's breath became increasingly unsteady as he fought off the wave of final ecstasy threatening to break. Only when Quinn found her release would he submit to his own.

He gripped her hips and slammed deep inside her. Once, twice, three times—he withdrew and repeated the rhythm. The white noise was building in his head, his muscles beginning to tremble as his climax drew ever nearer.

Quinn lifted her head from the pillows, her panting breath giving way to her cries of ultimate pleasure and he answered her call with one of his own. His body shook with all-encompassing relief as he gave himself completely to her. For that brief moment he experienced pure joy and imagined how it would be to have this feeling last. Making love to someone he was actually in love with was a game changer. He couldn't picture sharing his bed with anyone else again and that scared him half to death. The other half was willing to repeat the same mistake all over again.

He disposed of the condom and rolled onto the bed beside her, face first into the mattress, content to die here of exhaustion instead of having to get up again and face reality.

'What do we do now?' Quinn turned onto her side so he had a very nice view of her pert breasts.

'Try and breathe,' he said, unable to resist reaching out to cup her in his hand even through his exhaustion.

'I mean after that.'

He knew exactly what she meant but he didn't have the answer. At least, probably not the one she wanted to hear. She wanted to know what happened now they'd finally succumbed to the chemistry, to their feelings, but for him he couldn't let it change anything.

To enter into a full-blown relationship with Quinn entailed having one with Simon too. One which went beyond professional or friendship. He couldn't do that in good conscience when he could never be the father Simon needed. He wouldn't give him any more false hope.

He was done with the school runs, the birthday parties and the angsty teenage rebellion stage. Whilst he didn't regret being the sole provider for his sisters, he was too jaded and tired to go through it all again.

Yet, he was advancing ever further towards the vacancy.

'You're fostering Simon, right? Someday he'll be adopted and you'll start the process over with someone new?'

'Well…yes. The children are only placed temporarily in my care until a family can be found for them.' Quinn frowned at him and he could tell the idea of not having the boy around was already becoming a touchy subject. They'd both got in over their heads but Matt was determined he, at least, was going to keep swimming against the tide.

'What if we apply the same restriction to our relationship?' It was the only logical way this could continue without any one of them coming to serious harm.

'You want me to foster you too?' Quinn danced the flat of her hand down his back, over the curve of his backside and across his thigh until he was back to full fighting strength and falling for her blatant attempt to leave this discussion for another time.

'More of a co-dependency until you've found your for ever family too.' In his heart he couldn't let it go on once Simon left her. There could never be a future for them as a couple because there would always be a child in need and Quinn's heart was too open to deny anyone the love they craved.

It wouldn't be fair to stop her simply because his heart was closed for business.

She sighed next to him, the heavy resignation of the situation coming from deep within a soul still searching for its mate. It was too bad it couldn't be him, then his own wouldn't be howling at the injustice he was doing to it.

'I'm beginning to think that's an impossible dream.'

'You're a great foster mother, a beautiful woman and an incredible lover.' He traced his thumb across her lips, hating they were talking about the next man who'd get to kiss them.

'Yeah?' She coquettishly accepted his compliment and he was in danger of digging a hole in the mattress as his libido decided they should make the most of their time together in bed.

'Yeah, and I think we should make a few more memories so I never forget.' Not that it was likely.

Quinn was the one woman, other than his sisters, who'd ever truly touched his heart and gave his life more meaning simply by being in it. The same probably couldn't be said about him when he'd only be able to give her fun and sex at a time when she needed stability. When she looked back she'd see they'd muddled personal feelings with the intensity of Simon's treatment. What he didn't want was for her to end up hating him for taking advantage of her. If they kept it light, kept it fun, kept it physical, there'd be no need to get into the heavy emotional stuff he had no room for any more.

He threw an arm across Quinn and rolled onto his back, bringing her with him so she straddled his thighs. With her sex pressed against his, the logical side of his brain finally shut up.

Quinn wasn't stupid. Sex was Matt's way of avoiding deep and meaningful conversation. She didn't blame him. Nothing good was going to come of them in their case. When Simon left, so would he, if not sooner. At some point in the near future they'd both be gone, leaving nothing but memories and a void in her heart. It was much easier to take pleasure where she could find it in the here and now than face the prospect of that pain. She'd rather have this kind of procrastination than ugly crying over bridal magazines for a relationship that would never happen.

For every fake idyll that popped into her head of her and Matt and their foster brood, she ground her hips against him to block it out. The rush of arousal instantly channelled her thoughts to those of self-pleasure instead of an impossible dream.

With her hands braced on Matt's sturdy chest, she rocked back and forth. His arousal strengthened as she slid along his length so she took him in hand and guided him into her slick entrance, giving them both what they craved for now. They fit perfectly, snug, as if they'd both found their other halves.

Matt was watching her, his eyes hooded with

desire, but this time he was letting her make all the moves. Only thinking of herself for once, taking what she wanted, was kind of liberating. With a firm hand she teased the tip of his shaft along her folds until she was aching to have him inside her again. She anchored herself to him and that blessed relief soon gave way to a new need. Every circular motion of her hips brought another gasp of self-pleasure and a step closer to blinding bliss.

She doubled over, riding out the first shudders of impending climax. Matt sat up to capture one of her nipples with his mouth and sucked hard until it blurred the pleasure and pain barriers. Her orgasm came quickly and consumed her from the inside out, leaving her body weak from the strength of it.

Matt held her in place as he thrust upwards, finally taking his own satisfaction. Each time his hungry mouth found her breast or his deft fingers sought to please her again, another aftershock rippled through her. Only when she felt him tense beneath her, his grip on her tighten and the roar of his triumph ring in her ears did she finally let exhaustion claim her.

'That was…unexpected. Great, just…unexpected.'

As much for her as it was for him. She didn't recall ever being that confident in the bedroom before.

'I'm full of surprises, me.' She gave him a sly smile and hoped now he saw her as much more than a fragile foster mum he didn't want to be lumbered with for the rest of his days. There was still a sexy, independent-thinking, fun-loving woman inside her. She just hoped he assumed it was *her* husky voice he was hearing and not the raw-throated mutterings of a girl brought to the edge of tears by great sex.

He slung his arm around her shoulders and pulled her close. She didn't know how long they'd been locked away in this room, in their own world of fire and passion where time didn't matter. There was that residual parental guilt that perhaps she'd spent too long indulging her own needs while neglecting her son's but the warmth of Matt's skin against hers and the steady rhythm of his heart beating beneath her ear soon convinced her to stay here for a while longer. Simon was safe, and in Matt's arms, so was she.

'We'll pick Simon up once we've had a rest,' he mumbled into her hair.

Without prompting, Matt had raised the matter, something she'd been hesitant to do in case she ruined the moment. Her last thought as she drifted off to sleep was a happy one.

CHAPTER ELEVEN

'CAN I WALK HER? Please?' Simon hovered between Quinn and Matt, eyeing the dog's lead as if it was the hottest toy of the year.

Quinn glanced at Maisie's *official* owner for confirmation it was okay even though she and Simon walked her in the park practically every day.

'Sure.' Matt handed over control without a second thought. It was that kind of trust between him and Simon which was helping to build up the boy's confidence. That, and a hyperactive dog which kept them all too busy to dwell on any unpleasantness.

They'd fallen into a new routine, one which included exercising the dog and therefore getting Simon out and about in between hospital visits. Dare she say it, things had begun to settle down and they had so much going on now Simon's scars no longer seemed to be their main focus. Especially when those on his face were slowly beginning to fade.

As well as their dog-sitting duties, Quinn had the hospital committee meetings to attend and Simon was working towards his return to school. There'd been a phased return to classes held in the nearby hall, and although he'd been nervous, it had helped that some of his classmates were still being treated for minor injuries, including some burns. They understood what had happened to alter his appearance better than most but it didn't stop Quinn worrying.

'Hold on tight to Maisie's lead and don't go too far ahead,' she shouted after the enthusiastic duo haring through the park, although the sound of happy barking and childish laughter was music to her ears.

'They'll be grand. With any luck they'll tire each other out.' Matt cemented his place as the laid-back half of the partnership content to hang back and let the duo explore the wide open space, whist she remained the resident worrywart.

'Getting that dog was the best decision we could have made.' She knew pets were sometimes used as therapy for patients but she hadn't expected such impressive results so quickly. Simon was finally coming out of the shadows back into the light.

'Not *the* best decision.'

Quinn gave a yelp as he yanked her by the arm behind a nearby tree. He quietened her protest with his mouth. The kiss, full of want and demanding at first, soon softened, making her a slave to his touch. Okay, taking that long-awaited step into the bedroom had been one of the highlights of her year, perhaps even her lifetime. That in itself caused her more problems, as once would never be enough.

'We should really make sure those two aren't getting up to any mischief.'

'Like us?' He arched that devil eyebrow again, daring her to do something more wicked than snatching a few kisses out of sight.

She swallowed hard and tried to centre herself so she didn't get carried off into the clouds too easily.

'I hope not,' she muttered under her breath. If Simon was in a fraction of the trouble she was in right now she'd completely lose the plot.

'I want you.' Matt's growl in her ear spoke directly to her hormones, sending them into a frenzy and making her thankful she had a two-hundred-year-old oak tree to keep her upright.

These illicit encounters were all very exciting, but for someone as sexually charged as Matt, her inability to follow it through to the bedroom again would get old real quick.

Now that she'd discovered how fiercely hot their passion could burn, left unchecked there was nothing she'd enjoy more than falling into bed with him, but it was difficult to find enough Simon-free time to revel in each other the way they wanted to.

It was wrong to keep asking Mrs Johns to bab-ysit and she was afraid if she started sleeping over at Matt's she would have to inform the foster authorities of his involvement in her life. That meant forcing him into a commitment he'd been very clear he didn't want and could signal the end of the good thing they had going. No matter how frustrated she was waiting for some more alone time it had to be better than never seeing him again.

Matt grazed his teeth along her neck, gave her a playful nip, and she began to float away from common sense all over again.

A snuffling sound at her feet and a wet tongue across her bare toes soon grounded her. She should have known open-toed sandals were a bad move for a dog walk.

'Maisie?'

The dog apparently had a shoe fetish, having already chewed one of Matt's expensive work shoes and buried the other. It was just as well she was cute or she might have found herself back in doggie prison. Thankfully, Matt's soft spot for waifs and strays was greater than his affinity for Italian leather. Although it must have been a close call.

'Yay! She found you.' Simon came into view still attached to the other end of the lead and Quinn was quick to push Matt aside.

'She's a good tracker.' She bent down to rub Maisie's ears. It wasn't their canine companion's fault she didn't understand the necessity for discretion.

'Whatcha doin' here?' Simon tilted his head to one side as he assessed the scene.

'We...er—' She struggled for a cover story.

'Were playing hide and seek. You won.' Matt stepped in with a little white lie to save her skin. He could very well have told Simon the truth that they were together and stopped all of this pretence but that would entail following up with an *actual* relationship which involved sleepovers and paperwork. Perhaps Matt's eyes were open to all the baggage that she'd bring and he'd decided it wasn't worth the effort after all.

She had a horrible feeling their fragile relationship was already on the countdown to self-destruction.

'Is it our turn to hide?' Simon's eyes were wide

with excitement, the biggest smile on his face at the prospect of the game. It was going to be tough when it went back to being just the two of them.

She forced down the lump in her throat. 'Yup. We'll count to twenty and come and find you.'

Surely none of them could get into too much trouble in that short space of time?

She was rewarded with another beaming smile and a lick. Neither of which came from Matt.

'I'm as fond of a quickie as the next guy but twenty seconds? You wound me.' He clutched his chest in mock horror at the slight against his stamina.

That pleasure might seem like an age ago now but she could attest that it definitely wasn't a problem. She evaded eye contact and ignored the renewed rush of arousal as her body recalled the memory in graphic detail or they'd be in danger of losing Simon in the woods altogether.

'One...two...three...'

'You're killing me, you know.' He shook his head and from the corner of her eye Quinn saw him adjust the crotch of his trousers. A sight which was becoming more common with the increased rate of these passionate clinches. It wasn't fair on either of them.

'I don't mean to be a tease.' She gestured towards his groin area.

'I know but we really need to find a way to make this work.'

'Your penis?' She wanted to make him laugh, to steer the conversation away from that area of conflict they'd never be able to resolve satisfactorily.

It almost worked. He laughed at least.

'No, I'm fine in that department as you very well know. I mean us. We can't go on indefinitely hiding as though we're doing something wrong.'

'It's not as simple as clearing a space in my bathroom cabinet for your hair care products.' Her levity was waning as he made her face the reality of their situation.

'Of course. I'll require considerable wardrobe space too.'

'For an overnighter?'

'I do like a selection so I can dress according to my mood.'

Why couldn't life be as easy as their banter? Then perhaps her stomach wouldn't be tied up in knots waiting for the asteroid to hit and annihilate her world.

'All joking aside, we both know having you stay at my place, or us at yours, will only confuse Simon more than we already have. If we become an official couple I'll have to let the foster people know. I probably should've done that already but I didn't want to jinx this by putting it down on paper.'

The warmth of Matt's hands took the chill from her shoulders as he reassured her. 'As long as we're not signing a contract of intent I don't see why that should change things between us. It's understandable they'll want to protect Simon with background checks on anyone in his life but it's none of their business what our arrangement is. We can remain discreet where he's concerned. I'm the last person who wants him thinking I'm his replacement father. I can come over when he's asleep, leave before he's awake and make that time in between ours.'

She shivered, although there was no breeze in the air. It was a tempting offer, better than she expected in the circumstances. Yet there was something cold about the proposition. It snuffed out the last embers of hope that he'd ever want more than a physical relationship with her. Somewhere in her romantic heart she'd still imagined he could've been nudged further towards a more permanent role in their family. This was exactly the reason she'd wanted to keep Simon protected, because it was too late for her.

'That could work,' she said, not convinced it was the answer but the best one available for the moment.

At some point she was either going to have to push for more or sever all ties. Neither of which she was brave enough to do without prompting. The one consolation was that he was willing to stick around in some capacity and hadn't used this as an excuse to walk away. These days she took all the positives where she could find them and that new attitude had propelled her and Simon further forward than she could have hoped for.

Not that she was ready to admit it to anyone until she was one hundred percent sure it was the right thing to do, but she was thinking of making her and Simon's relationship more permanent. He was finally settling into her home, relaxing in her company and opening up to her. It wouldn't be fair to ask him to start all over again in a new town, with a new family and go to a school where they knew nothing of what he'd been through. Above everything else, she loved him as though he was her own son. He mightn't be of her flesh and blood, but she hurt when he hurt, cried when he cried, and seeing him happy again made her happy. They needed each other.

Adoption wasn't going to be straightforward, not even for a foster parent. She needed a bit more time to be certain it was right for both of them before she committed to the decision. There was no way she'd promise Simon a future if she thought she couldn't deliver. It would also be the end game for her and Matt.

His whole take on their relationship was based on the temporary nature of hers with Simon too. There was no way he'd stay involved once he found out she had ideas of becoming a permanent mum and all of the baggage that entailed. She wasn't ready to say goodbye to Matt either. For the meantime, it was better if the status quo remained the same.

'We'll talk it over later. When Simon's in bed.'

She would've mistaken his words for another wicked hint of what he wanted to do to her except he was taking her hand and leading her back towards Simon and the dog. It was his way of telling her he understood her concerns and was happy to comply. She swore her heart gave a happy sigh.

'Nineteen...twenty. Here we come, ready or not.'

Simon wasn't difficult to spot, his red jacket flashing in the trees and Maisie rolling in the grass beside him.

Quinn motioned for Matt to flank him from the far side whilst she approached from the other.

'Gotcha!' she said as she tagged him. It was only then she noticed his poor face streaked with tears.

'What's wrong, wee man?' Matt crouched down to comfort him too, as Quinn fought the urge to panic or beat herself up. She'd only left him for a few minutes.

'Are you hurt? Did you fall?' She rolled up his trousers searching for signs he'd cut himself or had some sort of accident.

He sniffed and shook his head. 'I thought you weren't coming for me.'

She was numb for the few seconds it took for the enormity of his fears to hit home. Simon longed for stability, had to be confident there'd be at least one person constant in his life taking care of his interests, or he'd never feel truly safe. Ready or not, it was her time to commit.

She hugged Simon tight and kissed the top of his head. 'I'm always going to be here for you. I love you very, very much and don't you ever forget it.'

Another sniff and a big pair of watery green eyes stared up at her.

'Thanks… Mum,' he said softly, as if testing the name on his lips. It almost had her sobbing along with him.

There was zero chance of her letting him go back into the system again without a fight. Whatever happened now, Simon was going to be the biggest part of her future and his happiness was her greatest reward.

She pulled him close again, channelling her love and hope for him in the embrace, and caught a glimpse of Matt's face over the top of his head as he joined in on the group hug. He was including himself in this moment of family unity when he could easily have stepped back and played no part in it. It was impossible not to let that flutter of hope take flight again when everything finally seemed to be coming together. She'd been brave enough to make that leap for Simon's sake and now it was Matt's turn to decide who, and what, he wanted.

* * *

It was a three-letter word—not the three little words Matt couldn't bring himself to say—which spelled the beginning of the end.

Mum.

He was happy for Quinn. It had been a beautiful moment watching them create a bond that nothing in this world could break. Including him. Not that he intended to come between them but he simply wasn't compatible with the new set-up. It was early days so it wasn't clear what role they expected him to play as the dynamics changed, but he was already becoming antsy about it.

Now they were back at Quinn's. She was putting Simon to bed, the dog was snoring by his feet and the scene would've been enough to content any family man. Except he wasn't a family man. Not with Quinn and Simon at least.

He enjoyed the lifestyle he had now. The one before they'd gatecrashed his apartment. He'd worked hard to gain his freedom and he wasn't about to trade it in for another unplanned, unwanted fatherhood. Some part of him had hoped that might change, that he might step forward and be the man they all needed him to be. Yet the overriding emotion he'd felt as they'd hugged wasn't happiness. That generally didn't bring on heart palpitations and an urge to run.

He was as fond of Simon as he was his own sisters and nieces and he was in love with Quinn, but it wasn't enough to persuade him to stay for ever. What if it didn't last anyway? He knew from experience his conscience wouldn't let him walk away from a child who counted on him for support and he didn't want to become emotionally tied to two families. It would be a step back and he wasn't afraid to admit he wasn't up to the job this time around if it meant saving everyone unnecessary pain later on.

Quinn tiptoed back downstairs from Simon's bedroom and curled up beside him on the settee. She rested her head on his chest the way she did most nights when they had five minutes together and yet tonight it seemed to hold more significance than he was comfortable with.

This wasn't about sex; it was about unwinding with each other at the end of the day, sharing the details of their struggles and triumphs. The companionship was becoming as important as the physical stuff, as were the emotions. Stay or go, it was going to hurt the same.

Her contented sigh as she cuddled into him reached in and twisted his gut. If only he was as settled there wouldn't be an issue but he was dancing over hot coals, afraid to linger too long and get burned.

'That was some day,' he said as he stroked the soft curtain of her hair fanned across his chest.

'Uh-huh. I never saw it coming. I mean, I was having a hard time thinking about him moving on but to hear him call me Mum—' Her voice cracked at the sentiment and Matt's insides constricted a little tighter.

'It's a big deal.'

'We'll have to get the ball rolling and make our intent known regarding the adoption. The sooner he knows this is his real home, the better.' She was full of plans, more invigorated by the breakthrough than Matt was prepared for.

'We?' Matt's fingers tangled in her hair, his whole body tense. This was exactly how he hadn't wanted this to play out.

'It's a figure of speech.' She sat bolt upright, eyes wide and watching his reaction. He wasn't that good an actor and neither was she. Slip of the tongue or not, Quinn didn't say things she didn't mean. She was already including him in the plans for Simon's future.

He leaned back, creating a healthy space between them so he could think clearly without the distraction of her softness pressed against him.

'Quinn—'

'Would it really be so bad though? I know we've danced around the subject but we *are* in a relationship, Matt. I need to know if you're behind me in this before we go any further.'

Nausea clawed its way through his system, his breathing shallow as the walls of his world moved in around him. He may as well be back living in that tiny council flat in Dublin where he'd barely enough room to breathe.

'Of course I'm behind you. I think adopting Simon will be good for you both.'

Quinn took a deep breath. 'I need to know if you're going to be part of it. I can't go through this again unless I know you're going to be with me one hundred percent. He's been through so much—neglected by his parents...abandoned by a foster family who'd promised him for ever—Simon needs, deserves, people willing to sacrifice everything for him. So do I.' She was braver than he, putting everything on the line and facing facts where he wasn't able to. It sucked that she was giving him a choice because then he had to make it.

'I just...can't.'

'But you already are. Don't you see? You're already part of our lives. All I'm asking is that you'll commit to us. I love you, Matt.'

The words she thought would fix everything only strengthened his case against this. It didn't matter who loved who because in the end they'd come to resent each other for it anyway. Love tied people together when the best thing could be for them to go their separate ways and find their own paths to happiness. Quinn and Simon would be better off without someone who'd learned to be selfish enough to want a life of his own.

'And what? Do you honestly think telling me that will erase my memory? I told you from the very start I didn't want anything serious. Adopting Simon sounds pretty damn serious to me. I told you I don't make promises I can't keep—that's why I was very sure not to make any.' Even as the words came out of his mouth he wanted to take them back, tell her he was sorry for being so harsh and take her in his arms again. He couldn't. Not when he was trying to make her see what a lost cause he was and how she'd be better off without him. He wanted her to hate him as much as he hated himself right now. It would be easier in the long run for her to move on by thinking he was capable of such cruelty when, actually, his own heart was breaking that this was over.

Quinn's blood ran cold enough to freeze her heart, Matt's words splintering it into tiny shards of ice.

It was happening all over again.

Just as she thought things were slotting into place, a man had to ruin everything.

Matt mightn't have verbally promised anything but the rejection hurt the same as any other. More so since she'd seen how he was around children, with Simon. They could've been great together if he'd only chosen them over his bachelorhood.

It didn't feel like it at the moment, but it was best she find out now he wasn't the man she thought he was than when Simon started calling him Dad.

Her son was her priority more than ever and she wasn't going to subject him to a string of fake relatives who'd dump them when they got tired of playing house. She couldn't be as logical in her thinking as Mr McGrory; her emotions would always get the better of her common sense.

'Yes, you were. How silly of me to forget you had a get-out clause.'

'Don't be like that, Quinn. We had a good time together but we both want different things.' He reached out to take her hand but she snatched it away. He didn't have the right to touch her any more and she couldn't bear it now she knew this was over. It hurt too much.

'We want you. You don't want us. Plain and simple. There's probably no point in drawing this out.' She unfurled her legs from beneath her to stand, faking a strength she didn't possess right now.

Matt took his time getting up. Contrary to every other night he'd been here, Quinn wanted him gone as soon as possible. She wanted to do her ugly crying and wailing in private. A break up was still painful whether you saw it coming or not and she needed a period of mourning before she picked herself up and started her new life over. One without Matt.

'I'll look into transferring Simon's care to another consultant.'

'No. I never wanted him to suffer as a result of our relationship. He deserves the very best and that's you. I think we can be grown-up enough to manage that. If not, I'll stay out of your way and let you get on with it.'

Appointments at the Castle were never going to be the same. The fairy tale was well and truly over but she hoped there was still some sort of happy-ever-after in sight even without her Prince Charming. She would miss his supporting role at the hospital as much as out of it. He'd got her through some of those darkest days but she couldn't force him to want to be around.

He nodded, his professional pride probably making the final decision on this one. 'Of course. There's no point in causing him any more disruption than necessary. We should probably make alternative arrangements for the dog too.'

She was the worst mother in the world, before she'd even officially been handed the title. Simon was going to lose his two best friends because she couldn't keep her emotions in check.

'Maybe you could email me your schedule and we'll work something out.'

She knew Matt didn't have the time, not really. The dog had been another pie in the sky idea that they hadn't fully thought through. Maisie was going to end up as another casualty of their doomed affair if they didn't take responsibility for their actions.

'You should take her. We got her for Simon's benefit after all, and it would prevent any... awkwardness.' He clearly wanted a clean break with no ties that weren't strictly professional.

The quick turnaround from an afternoon where he couldn't keep his hands off her was hard to stomach.

'I suppose if Simon's going to be here permanently there's no reason why we can't take her on.' Yet deep down she was still hoping for one just so there'd still be some sort of tenuous link between them.

Matt didn't appear to have any such sentimental leanings.

'I should go.' He turned towards the door, then back again, as if he wanted to say something more but didn't. Only an uneasy silence remained, giving her time to think about the days they'd had together, and those they wouldn't.

'Yes.' She'd always been too much for any man to consider taking on and there was no reason this time should've been any different. Now the last hope she'd had for a *normal* family had been pounded into dust, she had to make the most of the one she had. From here on in it was just her, Simon and Maisie.

She watched him walk away, telling herself she'd started this journey on her own and she was strong enough to continue without him.

The first tears fell before Matt was even out of sight.

He daren't look back. It had taken every ounce of his willpower to walk out of that door in the first place, knowing he was leaving her behind for good. Another glimpse of Quinn in warrior mode, those spiky defences he'd spent weeks breaking down firmly back in place, and he might just run back and beg for forgiveness. That wasn't going to solve anything even if it would ease his conscience for now.

She was a strong woman who'd be stronger without him, without putting her hopes in someone who could never be what she needed—a husband and a father for Simon. If he was out of the picture, at least in a personal capacity, they stood a better chance of a stable life and he, well, he could return to the spontaneity of his.

He pushed the button on the key fob to unlock the car door long before he reached it so he wouldn't start fumbling with it at the last minute and betray his lack of confidence in his decision-making. Once inside the vehicle he let out a slow, shaky breath. This was the hardest thing he'd ever done in his life because he'd *chosen* to walk away; it wasn't a decision forced upon him.

She'd told him she loved him. He loved her. It would have been easy to get carried away in the romance of the situation and believe they could all live happily ever after but real life wasn't as simple as that. Unfortunately, loving someone always meant sacrificing his independence, something he'd fought too hard for to let it slip away again so soon.

He started the car and sneaked a peek back at the house, hoping for one last glimpse of Quinn before he left. The door was already firmly shut, closing him out of her home for ever. He would still see her from time to time at the hospital but he was no longer part of her life. From now on Quinn, Simon and Maisie were no longer his responsibility. Exactly what he'd wanted. So why did he feel as if he'd thrown away the best thing that had ever happened to him?

CHAPTER TWELVE

'How are you, Simon?' It had been a couple of weeks since Matt's world had imploded. He'd taken a back seat, letting the nurses change the boy's dressings to give him time to get used to the idea he wasn't always going to be around.

It had been harder for Matt than he'd expected. Of course, he'd kept up to date on the boy's progress, interrogating the staff who'd treated him and scanning his notes for information. None of that made up for seeing him, or Quinn, in person.

He could operate and perform magic tricks for hundreds of other patients and their families but it wasn't the same. Apparently that connection they'd had was one of a kind and couldn't be replicated.

'Okay.' Simon eyed him warily as he'd done way back during the early stages of treatment as though trying to figure out if he could trust him or not. A punch to Matt's gut after all the time they'd spent together, and it was nobody's fault but his own.

He'd had a sleepless night with the prospect of this one-on-one today. Although Quinn had kept to her word and stayed out of sight whilst he did his rounds it didn't stop his hands sweating or his pulse racing at the thought she was in the building.

'How's Maisie?' he asked as he inspected the skin already healing well on Simon's face.

'Okay.'

He definitely wasn't giving anything away. Perhaps he thought sharing too much information was betraying Quinn in some way. It wasn't fair that he'd been stuck in the middle of all of this. Matt hadn't hung around for the nature of the break-up conversation between mother and son. It must've been difficult to explain his disappearance when they'd tried so hard to keep their relationship secret from him.

Simon's reluctance to talk could also be because he saw him as another father figure who'd abandoned him, in which case he'd every right to be mad at him. It was still important he trusted Matt when it came to his surgery.

'I miss her around the place, even though my shoes are safer without her.' He never would've imagined his place would be so lonely without the chaos, and he wasn't just talking about the dog.

'Is that why you don't want to see us any more? Did we do something wrong? I promise I won't let her eat any more of your stuff.'

The cold chill of guilt blasted through Matt's body and froze him to the spot. He couldn't let Simon think any of this mess was his fault when he'd been nothing but an innocent bystander dragged into his issues. They were his alone.

It was the earnest pools of green looking at him with pure bewilderment which eventually thawed his limbs so he could sit on the end of the hospital bed.

'What happened between me and Quinn…it wasn't because of anything you, or Maisie, did.

We've just decided it's better if we don't see each other.' This might've been easier if they'd co-ordinated their story at some point over these past weeks in case he contradicted anything he might've already been told.

At least Quinn mustn't have painted him as the bad guy if Simon thought he should some-how shoulder the blame. It was more than Matt deserved given his behaviour.

'Don't you like each other no more?'

If the situation had been as simple as Simon's point of view they would've still been together. He liked—loved—Quinn and she'd been fond of him enough to want him to be a part of their fam-ily. On paper it should've been a match made in heaven but he'd learned a long time ago that re-ality never matched up to rose-tinted daydreams.

'That's not really the problem.' As much as he'd tried, he couldn't switch off his feelings for Quinn. Not seeing her, talking to her or touch-ing her hadn't kept her from his thoughts, or his heart. In trying to protect himself he'd actually done more damage.

How could he explain to a five-year-old he'd lost the best thing that had ever happened to him because he was afraid of being part of a family again, or worse, enjoy it too much? The one thing he was trying to avoid was the ultimate goal for a foster kid.

'She misses you. Sometimes she's real sad when she thinks I'm not looking but she says she's going to be my new mummy and we'll have lots of fun together.'

It didn't come across as a ploy concocted to get Matt to break down and beg to be a part of it all again but he was close to breaking when Quinn was only a corridor away.

'I tell you what, after this surgery I'll have a chat with her and see if we can all go out for ice cream again some time.' They'd done the hardest part by making the break; meeting up for Simon's sake surely couldn't hurt any more than it already did. She still had Simon, and the dog, but the knowledge he'd saved himself from playing happy families didn't keep him warm at night.

The bribe did the trick of getting Simon back

onside again and prevented any further specu-
lation about what had happened. If Quinn had
a problem, well, she'd simply have to come and
talk to him about it.

He was just glad he and Simon were back on
speaking terms again. He was such a different
character from the withdrawn child he'd first en-
countered and Quinn was to thank for that. A
part of him wanted to believe he'd helped in some
small way too, aside from the cosmetic aspects.
Despite all of his misgivings about becoming too
involved, it was good to know it wasn't only his
heart which had been touched by their friendship.

He hadn't realised quite how much until they
were back in theatre, Simon asleep and completely at his mercy. For the first time in his career, Matt hesitated with the scalpel in his hand.

He would never operate on any of his sisters,
or his nieces, because he was too close, too emotionally involved, and that could mess with his
head. The consequences of something happening
to someone he loved because he wasn't thinking
clearly was a burden he could never live with.

Yet, here he was, hovering over a boy who'd come to mean so much to him, with a blade in his hand.

Simon *was* family, as was Quinn, and he'd abandoned them for the sake of his own pride. He'd always wondered how his life would've panned out if he'd shunned the responsibility thrust upon him to concentrate on his own survival. Now he knew. It was lonely, full of regret and unfulfilling without someone he loved to share it with.

His skin was clammy with the layer of cold realisation beneath his scrubs.

'Is everything all right?' One of the theatre assistants was quick to notice his uncharacteristic lapse in concentration.

'Yes.' He was confident in his response. He had to be. When he was in theatre he couldn't let his personal issues contaminate the sterile atmosphere.

He took a deep breath and let his professional demeanour sweep the remnants of his emotions to the side so he could do what was expected of him. It would be the last time he'd operate on Simon and he wasn't looking forward to breaking the news.

Quinn would never get used to the waiting. For some reason today seemed worse than all the other times Simon had been in surgery. The can't-sit-still fidgets were part parental worry and part running-into-an-ex anxiety.

With Matt still treating Simon it made an already stressful situation unbearable. There was no clean break like she'd had with Darryl. She hadn't seen him for dust once she'd insisted on going ahead with the fostering plan. This time she faced the prospect of seeing the man who'd broken her heart at every hospital appointment. She never knew which day might be the one she'd catch a glimpse of him to drive her over the edge.

Sure, things were going well with Simon in his recovery, and the adoption, but that didn't mean she could simply forget what she and Matt had had together. Could've had. She'd loved him and she was pretty sure he'd loved her, though he'd never said it and he hadn't been willing to trade in the single life for her. That was going to come back and haunt her every time she laid eyes on his handsome face. Out of Simon's sight, she'd cried, listened to sad songs and eaten gallons of ice cream straight from the tub but she hadn't reached the stage where she was ready to move on. She wasn't sure she ever really would.

No one got her like Matt; he seemed to know what she needed, and gave it to her, before she did. Except for what she'd wanted the most. Him. That's why it hurt so damn much. He'd known exactly what it would do to her by walking away; he'd told her long before she'd figured it out for herself. She could do the parenting alone, she just didn't want to.

For her, Matt had been the final piece of that family puzzle, slotting into place to complete the picture when there had been a void between her and Simon. Without him, she feared there'd always be a sense of that missing part of them and who knew where, or if, they'd ever be truly complete again. All she could do was her best to give

Simon a loving home and pray it could make up for everything else.

Missing boyfriend and father figure aside, Simon had been making great progress in terms of his recovery and schooling. Those days of being a *normal* mother and son no longer seemed so far out of reach. It was only on days such as this which brought home the memories of the fire and the extra worry she'd always shoulder for Simon's welfare.

The thumbs up from the nurses was always the cue she was awaiting so she could relax until he came around from the anaesthetic. This time her relief was short-lived as Matt came into view to add more stress to her daily quota.

'Did everything go to schedule?' It was the first time she'd spoken directly to him since they'd confronted the painful truth of their non-relationship so there was a flutter which made its way from her pulse to her voice. Worse, he was frowning, lines of worry etched deeply enough on her brow to put her on alert. Matt wasn't one to cause unnecessary drama on the wards and if he was worried about something it was definitely time to panic.

'Yeah. Fine...I need to talk to you.' He dropped his voice so other people couldn't hear and thereby induced a full-on panic attack.

It was never good news when doctors did that. Not when they were grabbing your arm and dragging you into a cubicle for a private word. Her heart was pounding so hard with fear, and being this close to him after such a long absence, she was starting to feel faint.

'What's happened? Is there an infection? I've tried to keep the dressings clean but you know what boys are like—' Her breathing was becoming rapid as she rattled through the possible disasters going on in her head.

Matt steered her towards the bed, forcing her to sit when the backs of her legs hit the mattress.

'He's fine. There were no problems or complication. I just can't treat him any more. I'm sorry but—'

The blood drained from her head to her toes and her limp body sank deeper into the bed.

The moment things seemed to be going well for Simon, she'd messed it up. She couldn't let him do this because of her. Simon needed him.

'Is it me? Next time I'll stay out of the way altogether. You don't even have to come onto the ward. I'll talk to the nurses or I can get Mrs Johns to bring him to his appointments. I'll do whatever it takes. I don't want to be the one to mess this up.'

Any further resolutions he had for the problem were silenced as Matt sealed her lips with his. The stealth kiss completely derailed her train of thought, leaving her dazed and wanting more. She touched her fingers to her moist lips, afraid it had been a dream conjured up by falling asleep in the corridor.

'What was that for?' she asked, almost afraid of the answer.

'It was the only way to shut you up so I could finish what I was saying. Well, probably not the only way, but the best one I could think of.' He was grinning at her, that mischievous twinkle in his eye sending tremors of anticipation wracking through her body, but she still didn't know what there was to smile about.

'But why? Why would you feel the need to kiss me after dumping me and then telling me you're dumping Simon too? It doesn't make any sense. Unless this is your idea of a sick joke. In which case I'm really not amused.' Her head was spinning from his bombshell, from the kiss and from the way she still wanted him even after everything he'd done.

'Do I need to do it again to get you to listen?' He was cupping her face in his hands, making direct eye contact so she couldn't lie.

'Yes,' she said without hesitation, and closed her eyes for one last touch of him against her lips.

Whatever the motive, she'd missed this. She hated herself for being so weak as she sagged against him and let him take control of her mouth, her emotions and her dignity when she should be railing against him for putting her through hell.

Although she kissed him back, she remained guarded, wary of getting her hopes up that this

was anything more than a spontaneous lapse of
his better judgement. Once the pressure eased
from the initial flare of rekindled passion, she
broke away.

'What's this about, Matt?'

He raked his hand through his hair before
crouching down so they were at eye level.

'I've missed you so much.'

Her stomach did a backflip and high-fived
her heart but she kept her mouth shut this time.
Words and kisses didn't change anything unless
they were accompanied by a bit of honesty. She
wasn't going to fall into that same trap of hoping she could change a man and make him want
to be a permanent fixture in her life. In fact, she
might draft that into a contract for future suitors
so she could weed out potential heartbreakers.
Although a Matt-replacement seemed a long way
off when the real one was still capable of upsetting her equilibrium to this extent.

'I can't do Simon's surgery any more because
I'm too close, too emotionally involved. It's
a conflict of interests and one which means I

have to choose between my personal and professional roles.'

'I don't understand. You're *choosing* not to treat him. Why is this supposed to be good news?' As far as she could see he was simply kicking them when they were down.

'I'm choosing you. If you'll still have me? Seeing Simon today in that theatre…it was like watching my own son go under the knife. It made me realise I'm already part of this family. I love you, Quinn. Both of you.'

She was too scared to believe he was saying what she thought he was saying. There'd been weeks of no communication from him and heartache for her and somehow now all of her dreams were coming true? She wasn't so easily fooled by a great smile and hot kisses any more. Maybe.

'What's changed, Matt? The last time we saw each other you were telling me the very opposite. Are you missing the dog or something? I'm sure we can make arrangements for a visit without forcing you into another relationship.' Okay, she was a little spiky but she'd every right to be after he'd ripped her heart out and she'd spent an age trying to patch it back up. If she meant anything to him he'd put up with a few scratches as he brushed against her new and improved defences.

The frown was back; she might have pushed him a tad too far.

'That's what I'm trying to tell you. I miss you all. This time apart has showed me what I'm missing. I don't want to end up a lonely old man with nothing but expensive furniture and fittings to keep me company. I've seen a glimpse of what life is like without you and Simon and it's not for me. I love you. I want to be with you, raising Simon, or a whole house full of Simons if that's what you want.'

'There's nothing I want more but only if that's truly what you want this time. How can I be sure you won't change your mind when the adoption comes through or there's another troubled kid on the doorstep? There can't be any room for doubt, Matt.' She pushed back at the flutter of hope beating hard against her chest trying to escape and send her tumbling back into Matt's arms.

He stood up, paced the room with his hands on his hips, and she knew she'd called his bluff.

'That's what I thought,' she said as she got to her feet, her voice cracking at the joyless victory.

'Wait. Where are you going?'

'To see Simon.' He was the only reason she hadn't completely fallen apart. She had to be the strong one in that relationship and he'd need her when he woke up and heard the latest bad news.

Matt stepped quickly into the path between her and the door to prolong her agony a while longer.

'What if I move in with you? Would that convince you I'm serious? I'll quit my lease, sell everything. I'll take a cleaning job at the hospital if it means I can stay on. I don't care about any of it. I just want to be with you.'

That made her smile.

'I think the hospital would give anything to keep you here given the chance.'

'And you?' He had that same worried look Simon had when he thought she didn't want him and in that moment she knew he meant every word. He was laying himself open here and this level of honesty was simply irresistible.

'Well, you know I'm a sucker for a stray so

I guess I'll keep you too.' It was easier to joke when she was secure in his feelings for her.

'Tell me you love me.' He gathered her into his arms, a smile playing across his lips now too.

'You're so needy.'

'Tell me,' he said again, his mouth moving against hers.

'I love you.' She'd tried to convince herself otherwise since he'd left but it was a relief to finally admit it aloud without fearing the consequences.

'I love you too. And Simon. And Maisie. And this mad, dysfunctional family we've created.'

'I think there's someone else who's going to be very happy to hear the news.'

'Let's go get our boy.' Matt took her hand and led her towards Simon's room to complete the group love-in.

Quinn's heart was so full she didn't think she'd ever stop smiling.

Now her family was finally complete.

* * * * *

Welcome to the
PADDINGTON CHILDREN'S HOSPITAL
six-book series

Available now:

THEIR ONE NIGHT BABY
by Carol Marinelli
FORBIDDEN TO THE PLAYBOY SURGEON
by Fiona Lowe
MUMMY, NURSE... DUCHESS?
by Kate Hardy
FALLING FOR THE FOSTER MUM
by Karin Baine

Coming soon:

HEALING THE SHEIKH'S HEART
by Annie O'Neil
A LIFE-SAVING REUNION
by Alison Roberts